THE LOOK OF LOVE

THE LOOK OF LOVE

MARY JANE CLARK

WM
WILLIAM MORROW
An Imprint of HarperCollins*Publishers*

This book is a work of fiction. References to real people, events, establishments, organizations, or locales are intended only to provide a sense of authenticity, and are used fictitiously. All other characters, and all incidents and dialogue, are drawn from the author's imagination and are not to be construed as real.

HarperCollins books may be purchased for educational, business, or sales promotional use. For information please write: Special Markets Department, HarperCollins Publishers, 10 East 53rd Street, New York, NY 10022.

FIRST EDITION

Designed by Jamie Lynn Kerner

Library of Congress Cataloging-in-Publication Data has been applied for.

ISBN 978-0-06-199556-9

11 12 13 14 15   OV/RRD   10 9 8 7 6 5 4 3 2 1

For Elizabeth and David, my two incredible blessings.
I am so proud of both of you.
And for all those who struggle with Fragile X Syndrome
as clinical trials for a treatment are under way.

THE LOOK OF LOVE

PROLOGUE

SHE OFTEN WALKED FROM ROOM to room, pretending the place was hers. This fantasy never failed to help her get through the hours of dusting, scrubbing, and vacuuming. Esperanza imagined what it would feel like to own a huge, beautiful house like this instead of being the woman hired to clean it once a week.

As she returned the broom to the kitchen closet, she told herself that this was as good as any housekeeping job could be. The owner was very neat and spent most of her time at work or with her fiancé. Some weeks Esperanza could tell by the perfectly plumped pillows and the lack of footprints on the carpet that Jillian Abernathy had never even entered a room since the last time it had been cleaned.

Still, dust accumulated, silver tarnished, and windows got dirty. Esperanza kept on top of every chore and prided herself on the fact that Jillian had never left a note about something that had been missed or reminding Esperanza of a task left undone. She tried to see it all through Jillian's eyes and anticipate the way Jillian would want things. She did everything she could think of to satisfy Jillian.

How she wished she *were* Jillian.

Though Esperanza was born in the United States, her parents had been illegal Mexican immigrants. Her father had been a day laborer with landscapers and contractors. Her mother did housework herself.

But Esperanza longed to live the real American dream. How fabulous to be beautiful and rich, to have a father who operated on the faces of other wealthy people and owned one of the most luxurious spas in America, to have a handsome fiancé who was also a doctor. It would be amazing to live and work every day in lush surroundings, wear designer clothes, and have your employees bend over backward to please you. It would be fantastic *not* to have to clean other people's toilets. Esperanza went to the dining room and began straightening the boxes stacked in the corners and accumulated on the table and sideboard, packages representing stores she had seen only from the outside when she got up the nerve to walk along Rodeo Drive. She peeked at the wedding gifts she recognized as new arrivals since last week: sterling-silver flatware and crystal glasses from Tiffany's, bed linens from Frette, a Lladró figurine, Hermès towels.

She was momentarily startled as she caught a glimpse of herself in the mirror that hung over the sideboard. Esperanza still wasn't used to seeing herself as a blonde. Though the box of hair color she'd purchased at the drugstore hadn't transformed her jet-black hair into the various golden shades of Jillian's, it was close enough.

Satisfied that all was in order, Esperanza hurried down the hall. She liked doing Jillian's room last. It was her reward, the high point of her workday. Sometimes Jillian left a shopping bag for her on the bed containing a barely worn pair of shoes or a seemingly brand-new purse she didn't want anymore. But today there was nothing.

Esperanza shrugged as she headed to her favorite spot in the house: Jillian's walk-in closet. She opened the double doors, looked inside, and gasped. Hanging from the middle of the ceiling was the most beautiful dress she had ever seen. As she reached out to gently touch the frothy white taffeta ruffles cascading down the A-line skirt, the thought crossed her mind.

Unable to resist, Esperanza peeled off her clothes and carefully took the gown from the satin-padded hanger. She stepped into the dress and pulled it up over her body. She was a bit bustier than Jillian, and her breasts strained against the sweetheart neckline. Other than that, the dress fit her almost perfectly.

She spied a pair of white silk-and-lace high heels perched on the shelf. Taking them down, she slipped them on her feet. She was preening and admiring herself in the full-length mirror when she heard the buzzer. Esperanza gathered up the skirt of the gown and hurried to the intercom.

It was a messenger delivering another wedding gift.

"Just a minute," she said. "I'll be right there."

3

She kicked off the shoes, then took off the dress and meticulously laid it out on the bed. Pulling a robe from the hook on the closet door, she wrapped it around herself and hurried down the hall. Her heart pounded in her chest. She was relieved it was only a messenger. What if it had been Jillian? What if she'd been caught?

Reaching the foyer, Esperanza was thinking of how quickly she wanted to get back to Jillian's bedroom and restore everything to the way it was. As she opened the front door, she caught only a glimpse of dark sunglasses and a blue cap before the burning liquid hit her face and she began to scream in agony.

CHAPTER

1

NEW YEAR'S EVE

THE OFFER SEEMED ALMOST TOO good to be true.

Round-trip airfare to Los Angeles and an all-expenses-paid stay at one of the most luxurious spas in the country. But there *was* a catch: Piper Donovan had to make another wedding cake.

Distracted from selecting her ensemble for the party she was going to that night, Piper pushed aside the dresses, skirts, and tops strewn all over her bed. She lay down on the soft comforter, crossed her long, thin legs and scrolled her BlackBerry to where she could reread the Facebook message.

SAW THE CAKE YOU MADE FOR GLENNA BROOKS. WOULD LOVE IT IF YOU WOULD DO ONE FOR MY WEDDING ON JANUARY 15.

WE'LL PAY FOR YOUR PLANE TICKET, PUT YOU UP FOR THE
WEEK AT ELYSIUM, PROVIDE YOU WITH A CAR AND DRIVER,
AND, OF COURSE, PAY FOR THE CAKE. LET ME KNOW ASAP IF
YOU ARE INTERESTED!

Jillian Abernathy. The name was vaguely familiar.

Piper studied the photo that accompanied the message.
An attractive young couple beamed from the screen. The
woman was pretty and blond, and she had a dazzling white
smile. The handsome man, with his arm around her, had
dark hair, and his teeth were even more blinding. Click-
ing on the picture led to Jillian Abernathy's Facebook pro-
file. Her info page revealed that Jillian was engaged to Ben
Dixon, M.D., and that she worked as the director of the Elysium Spa.

Piper wondered where Jillian had first seen the three-
tiered, star-festooned cake she'd designed for soap-opera star
Glenna Brooks. There were photos of it all over the Internet,
and it was featured in the current issues of *People, Soap Opera
Weekly,* and the *National Enquirer,* along with other pictures
from the wedding and accompanying text explaining the di-
sasters that had befallen co-workers of the bride and groom
in the weeks leading up to the ceremony. Piper had posted
pictures of her creation on her own Facebook fan page, and
the response had been overwhelming. She was proud of her
first wedding cake and stunned by the attention it had been
receiving since the Christmas Eve nuptials. She hadn't expected to be making another so quickly—or all by herself.

She'd had her mother as a safety net while she worked on Glenna's cake.

Piper was dying to tell her mother, but Terri Donovan was still at the bakery and wouldn't be home for a few hours. Piper stared at the freshly painted, cloyingly pink walls of her room in her parents' house and considered the offer. She'd been living home again for just a month, yet the idea of getting away for a while was appealing. She loved her parents—she did—but there was something wrong about being twenty-seven years old and having to answer to them. Piper knew that Terri and Vin Donovan were making a concerted effort not to smother her, but they were failing miserably. It was inevitable: Piper was their only daughter, their baby, and they still found her every move fascinating. They paid attention to everything she did—or at least everything they *knew* she did.

"Hey, Emmett! Drop that! Drop that right now!" Piper yelled, jumping up from the bed and lunging for the Jack Russell terrier. The little dog had the toe of one of Piper's high-heeled pumps grasped firmly in his mouth. He looked at her, dropped the shoe, and ran from the room.

She picked up the black pump and inspected it. There were tooth marks in the leather, but there was no actual tearing. Maybe her father could figure out a way to smooth away the indentations. He could fix pretty much anything.

Piper thought more about accepting the job. Even though she'd have to design and make the wedding cake, she would still have some free time. Maybe her agent, Gabe

Leonard, could get her an audition or two while she was out there. Weather-wise, Southern California was decidedly better than New Jersey in January. And the idea of some free beauty treatments was definitely alluring.

Who wouldn't want to spend a week at Elysium? Piper had read about the oasis perched in the Hollywood Hills. She even knew a few people who had checked in there for some high-priced pampering. She'd listened as seldom-impressed New Yorkers used adjectives like "divine" and "heaven" to describe it. Apparently the staff went through Swiss Guard–like training to learn how to cater to each client's well-being.

Going online, Piper read more. Besides the usual massages, facials, body wraps, yoga, Pilates, meditation sessions, saunas, and hot-tub soaks, Elysium offered individualized consultations with dietitians, along with organic, vegetarian, and vegan dining. It also boasted personal touches like spritzing clients with Evian as they lounged by an infinity pool that offered an aerial view of Los Angeles. All these amenities had guests leaving relaxed, rejuvenated, and feeling that every penny they'd spent had been worth it.

Elysium also provided its clients the most luxurious thing in the world—privacy. For good reason: The owner of Elysium was a renowned cosmetic surgeon. Along with the sprawling Spanish Mission–style main building that housed most of the guests in private rooms, there were individual cottages scattered in a more secluded section of the property. Actors, politicians, and other celebrities, both male and female—as well as those who could afford it and wanted no one to know they were being "freshened up"—arrived, had their surgery, and recuperated in utmost secrecy.

Piper exited Elysium's Web site, picked up the damaged shoe, and headed downstairs. When she reached the basement of the split-level she had grown up in, Piper found her father ensconced in his man cave, surrounded by his beloved workbench, tools, and "survivor" paraphernalia. He was watching a football game on the little television set he kept down there. She handed him the shoe for his inspection.

"It's Emmett or me!" said Piper, offering the fake ultimatum for the umpteenth time.

"That dog is a devil," said Vin, shaking his head and trying to keep the smile from his face. Her father acted tough, but Piper and her mother knew he was a sucker for the dog. He got a kick out of the mischievous things the terrier did.

Piper sank into an old couch that had found its way into the basement when a new one had taken its place in the living room. She watched as her father worked on the shoe.

"Guess what?" she asked.

"What?" Vin was busy rubbing the black leather with a soft cloth.

"Somebody wants me to make another wedding cake." Piper looked at her father for his reaction.

"Oh, yeah?" His eyes remained trained on the toe of the pump.

"The bride saw the cake I made for Glenna and was

really into it, so she wants to hire me to make hers." Piper pulled a long blond hair from the shoulder of her sweater.

"That's nice, lovey." Vin turned the shoe and began working on it from another angle.

"She'll pay for me to go out to California."

Vin lowered the shoe and turned to look at his daughter. "You're kidding me."

Piper nodded, her green eyes sparkling. "Not bad, huh?"

"What are you going to say?" asked Vin. "Do you want to do it?"

Piper shrugged. "Yeah, I think I do. I mean, I don't have anything going on here right now. And with a little luck, my agent might be able to send me on some go-sees while I'm there. You know there are, like, four or five acting jobs out there for every one in New York."

"And where would you stay?" asked Vin.

"That's the best part," said Piper. "The bride is the director of Elysium, which is this legendary Hollywood spa. I can stay there all week. I'll have to check, but I assume I'll be able to use their kitchen."

Vin's eyes narrowed. "I know about Elysium."

"You do?" asked Piper.

Vin handed the shoe to his daughter. All traces of Emmett's bite had been erased.

"Yes," said Vin. "And I think I know about your bride, too."

"Jillian Abernathy? How would you know about her?"

"Because I watch the news, Piper," said Vin, in a tone that made it clear that he thought Piper should, too. "Jillian Abernathy is one lucky gal. She wasn't home when some nutjob showed up at her front door. The poor cleaning woman answered the bell and got a cupful of acid, smack in the face."

CHAPTER

2

JILLIAN ABERNATHY BRACED HERSELF, AS she always did, before entering Cottage 7. She'd been tempted to skip today's visit. She still had to stop at the market for something to grill, and she also wanted to pick up a bottle of champagne. She and Ben were going to stay in and spend a quiet evening together.

She had no desire to go to some noisy party or club. The last thing she wanted was to mingle with a New Year's Eve crowd. Not only because she didn't think it was appropriate to be out celebrating, but because she was scared that somebody could get close and hurt her.

In the months since the acid attack on Esperanza, Jillian had been afraid to go to work each morning, in spite of the security service her father had hired to keep watch outside her home. She found herself constantly checking to make sure that the doors and windows were locked. Sudden noises made her jump. Though Jillian hadn't been the one harmed, the police seemed certain that the attack had been meant for her. The thought left her terrified.

The assault had changed everything. The wedding had been postponed. It just didn't seem right to go on with it until things settled down. Esperanza was suffering so much pain, physically and emotionally. It was best to concentrate on restoring her to health.

After Esperanza's stay in the hospital and the preliminary surgeries, Jillian's father had insisted that she recuperate in one of the private cottages at Elysium. He was also doing further cosmetic surgeries to repair her face, at no charge. If there was anything to be grateful for, it was that while the acid had burned the bottom half of Esperanza's face, it had missed her eyes.

The media attention had been suffocating. The story of the acid attack was sensational enough on its own, but the fact that the disfigured cleaning woman worked for the daughter of the wealthy Abernathy family, owners of the famed Elysium, temple to beauty, added irony and extra fascination to the news coverage. Jillian had lived in a constant state of tension, never knowing when a reporter was going to accost her or a camera crew was going to be staked outside her house. Many nights she stayed in a cottage at Elysium, where she could have more privacy and feel more protected.

It hadn't been until Christmas Day, as her gift to Ben,

that Jillian finally agreed to go ahead with the wedding, as long as it could be done quickly and on a much smaller scale than the celebration they'd originally planned. The guest list was being cut dramatically. Instead of a cathedral wedding ceremony and a reception at the opulent Beverly Hills Hotel, Jillian wanted all of it to happen on the grounds of Elysium, where everything could be controlled by their own trusted staff.

As she approached the front door of the terra-cotta-roofed cottage, Jillian could hear the television playing inside. A gauzy curtain fluttered through a slightly open window. She peeked in and saw Esperanza engrossed in the show on the screen, sitting with her back to the window. Esperanza's shoulders moved jerkily up and down, and Jillian realized she was actually laughing, or her version of it. Laughing silently, not moving her mouth or her facial muscles.

Jillian stepped away from the window and knocked on the cottage door.

"Who is it?" called Esperanza from inside. The words were not distinctly pronounced.

"It's me. Jillian." She arranged her face in a smile and girded herself for what she would see. The door opened.

"Hello, miss."

Esperanza was wearing a peach-colored smock. Her hair was long and dark, with only the last vestige of yellow at the ends. The bottom of her face was covered with a clear plastic mask, modeled expressly for her and fitting directly against her ravaged skin. The mask applied direct pressure over the wounds to help prevent the buildup of collagen fibers that could scar and to protect the skin from any forces that could impair the healing process. Jillian knew that the face covering provided a barrier from germs and irritants and allowed visual inspection without having to be removed. So, all in all, the mask was a very good thing. Still, it always reminded Jillian of something a thief or a rapist or a home invader might wear to grotesquely distort his facial features. She shivered every time she saw it.

"How are you feeling today, Esperanza?" asked Jillian as she walked inside the cottage.

Esperanza picked up the remote, pointed it at the television, and turned down the sound. She gestured to her face as she settled into her chair. "I felt pretty good this morning, but now it's hurting again."

Jillian nodded as she took a seat on the sofa. "In the morning you're rested and have more energy. Later in the day, your body is tired and things bother you more. Do you want me to call and have them bring you something for the pain?"

Esperanza gently shook her head. "No thank you, miss. I'll wait until it's time for my sleeping medicine."

"Good for you," said Jillian. She leaned forward and patted the woman's knee. "I know you don't want to get too dependent on the pain medication, Esperanza. I admire you for that, but drugs are there to help. You don't have to worry. Our doctor is very careful about monitoring how much is available to you."

Jillian noticed that Esperanza was wearing the gold bangle bracelet Jillian had given her for Christmas. She also noticed that Esperanza's nails were freshly manicured and painted with cheerful red polish—the hands of a woman who no longer did housework for a living. Esperanza looked down and fiddled with the corner of her smock.

"What's the matter?" asked Jillian. "Is something wrong?"

"Nothing is wrong, miss. Everyone is so nice to me. They work so hard to help me and make sure I am comfortable. Tonight they are bringing me a special dinner for New Year's Eve." Esperanza's eyes smiled above the plastic mask.

"We have a lot to celebrate this year," said Jillian. "You've been healing so well. My father thinks he's going to be able to discharge you in a week or so. Isn't that wonderful, Esperanza? Soon you'll be able to go home to your own place."

ESPERANZA WATCHED THROUGH THE WINDOW until Jillian was out of sight. Then she went to the bedroom, climbed into the queen-size bed, and snuggled beneath the light down coverlet and freshly laundered white sheets.

She was torn. Of course she was glad that her healing was progressing and that Dr. Abernathy was confident that repeated procedures would continue to improve her appearance. But she didn't want to leave Elysium. She didn't want to go home.

Not ever.

After living in the luxury of Elysium, where the staff catered to her every desire, how could she return to the seedy and suffocating one-bedroom apartment she used to share with three other women? Actually, she couldn't go back there even if she wanted to return. She had given up her spot, and someone else had taken her place.

Esperanza wiggled her toes and felt the softness of the bed linens. She closed her eyes and began to concentrate on her breathing as the yoga teacher who came to the cottage for private lessons had taught her to do in order to relax. As she inhaled, a light scent of lavender filled her nostrils.

She loved it here.

Maybe if she told them that she was having flashbacks and was afraid for her life, they would see she was traumatized and let her stay longer. Esperanza hadn't told anyone that she was remembering something she saw when she opened the door and the acid was flung in her face. But she didn't want to answer any more questions from the police. Things had finally quieted down, and she didn't want to stir it all up again.

Most of all Esperanza was terrified that if threatened with identification, whoever had attacked and scarred her would find her and finish the job. Yet with what she now remembered, she realized that she might not really be safe at Elysium after all.

CHAPTER

3

Sister Mary Noelle bowed her head and knelt in the chapel of the Monastery of the Angels. Her fingers rubbed her rosary beads as she murmured the Hail Marys along with the voices she could hear praying on the other side of the screen that separated the chapel's two parts—one for the cloistered sisters and one for the laypeople who came to pray. They asked for various things: a job, the restoration of a damaged relationship, a cure for a sick child, a miracle.

She couldn't see them, and they couldn't see her.

Sister was aware that this was the most secular night of the year. Outside the monastery walls, traffic buzzed along the Los Angeles freeways. People were heading off to an evening of partying and drinking, often to excess. Glamorous clothes and makeup, gyrating bodies, bright lights, dreams of being discovered by modeling agents or casting directors beckoned.

For Sister Mary Noelle, the beckoning had come from Christ, when he asked her to "Come follow me." That beckoning had led her to the contemplative life of a cloistered nun. She had completed her two years as a postulant, taken her simple vows, and was now a novice extern sister, with two more years until she made her final vows.

It was a life she would never have imagined for herself as she grew up just a few miles away, the daughter of a successful plastic surgeon and a former model and actress. She and her sister had lived a beautiful life, in a beautiful home, and they'd gone to private schools where they socialized with other beautiful people. She grew up thinking that was just the way it should be. She had been proud of her father and the things people said about him, the way they raved about his work and declared him a miracle worker. The magazine articles about the spa he had founded touted his "magic hands." The tabloids speculated on various movie stars for whom her father had turned back time. Occasionally she'd overheard her father telling her mother about the actor or actress who had come to Elysium looking to be transformed in order to revive a flagging career.

"Hail Mary, full of grace, the Lord is with thee." Sister Mary Noelle's lips moved, but barely a whisper came out of her mouth. She prayed for her dear father, her beloved sister, and her deceased mother.

Sometimes through the greatest pain came the greatest

blessings. If her mother hadn't died of a heart attack after cosmetic surgery, Sister Mary Noelle might never have rejected the empty pursuit of physical beauty. She might never have discovered what was truly important. She might never have become Sister Mary Noelle.

CHAPTER

4

BEFORE SHE DRESSED FOR THE party, Piper took a minute to Google the name Jillian Abernathy. The most recent links were to articles about the acid attack. They recounted that a woman, hired to clean the house, had opened Jillian's front door thinking she'd be accepting delivery of a gift for her employer's upcoming wedding. The victim was unable to provide a description of the attacker, recalling only that she did catch a glimpse of a pair of aviator sunglasses and a blue cap before the acid was thrown in her face.

Esperanza Flores, thirty-one, was quoted from an interview conducted in her hospital room. "I couldn't stop screaming. My face was on fire. The worst fire you can imagine."

The case remained unsolved. As Piper searched further, she came upon older stories. One headline read BUSINESS

MAJOR HITS THE GROUND RUNNING. The article explained that immediately after graduation from USC, Jillian had taken over as director of Elysium, replacing Hudson Sherwood. Sherwood had been Elysium's director since the spa was founded by Jillian's father.

Nepotism at its best, thought Piper.

There were several articles about Elysium in which Jillian was quoted. All of them seemed to be puff pieces, listing the fabulous treatments and amenities offered at the spa. Piper noticed that little mention was made of the cosmetic surgery done there.

Piper was about to log off when she spotted one last thing. It was a death notice that had run in the *Los Angeles Times* several years earlier. It listed Jillian Abernathy as one of the two daughters of Caryn Abernathy, formerly the actress Caryn Collins. No cause of death was listed.

Piper didn't recognize the name. She glanced at the clock and decided she'd have to learn more about Caryn Collins later. She had promised Jack she'd get to his place early to help him before the guests began arriving.

WHILE THE TRAFFIC AT THE George Washington Bridge was not too horrific, the FDR Drive was a nightmare. *Should have gone down the West Side Highway and cut over,* Piper thought as the cars inched along for over eighty blocks. When she got off at Twenty-third Street, she was already an hour late.

As she locked the sedan door, her BlackBerry rang. Feeling the cold air whipping across from the East River, Piper put the tray and the two shopping bags she was carrying on the hood of the car and pulled her handheld from the pocket of her coat. She glanced at the screen.

It was Jack.

"Hey, where are you?" he asked. She could hear the concern in his voice.

"I'm here," said Piper. "The traffic was horrible, but some guy was pulling out across the street from your building and I just got his space."

"Good. Do you need me to come down and help you with anything?"

"No, I can handle it," said Piper, eyeing the icy slush covering the stretch of pothole-ridden macadam that separated her from Peter Cooper Village. She wished her feet were encased in her warm, soft Uggs instead of the open, strappy shoes she'd gotten a pedicure to wear. "I'll be right up. Is anyone else there yet?"

"A few people."

"I'm so sorry I'm late, Jack."

"Forget it. Just come."

When she entered Jack's apartment, Piper saw that more than a few people had arrived. The place was already crowded. She didn't recognize most of the faces as she scanned the area, but she knew that many of them were men and women who worked with Jack at the FBI.

"My mother pretty much sent everything left over at the end of the day from the bakery," said Piper, putting down the tray and shopping bags with the ICING ON THE CUPCAKE logo emblazoned on the sides. Jack was standing at the counter in the tiny kitchen, opening a bottle of wine.

"Way to go, Terri! Thank her for me," said Jack as he leaned over to give Piper a kiss on the cheek. "Glad you're here."

"What can I do?" she asked, taking off her coat.

"Whoa," said Jack, his eyes sweeping up and down her body. "You can just stand exactly where you are and look like that all night. No, go out into the living room and stand in the middle of the rug so *everybody* can see you."

She smoothed the fabric of her short black skirt and adjusted the glittery, sleeveless emerald green top she'd chosen because it brought out the color of her eyes. Gold bangle bracelets decorated her well-toned arms. Her blond hair fell long and loose around her shoulders.

Piper smiled. "Stop, you're making me blush."

"Please, you love it. And if you can't agree that you look absolutely gorgeous tonight, then you're *never* gonna believe it."

PASSING TRAYS OF PIGS IN a blanket, cheese puffs, and bacon-wrapped scallops, Piper had the opportunity to mingle and meet Jack's friends. Every one of them recognized her name when she identified herself.

"So you're the famous Piper. Jack is always talking about you," said one man.

"Wow, Jack finally got something right. You *are* as pretty as he said you were," said another.

Piper was unprepared when one inebriated guy took hold of her arm and asked, "Why don't you two get a room already?"

As she wriggled free from his grasp, Piper could feel her cheeks grow hot. Instinctively, she looked around the room for Jack. She spotted him in the corner, laughing with a group. She'd thought about it—that was for sure.

Jack and she were just friends, weren't they? She'd been getting the feeling that he wanted more. Now his friends had pretty much confirmed that.

Piper was uncomfortable with the idea. Her own wedding had been called off seven months before. She hadn't been the one who'd done the canceling. It wasn't that she was still in love with Gordon. In fact, when she thought about the whole thing, which was less and less often, she realized that there were many reasons it hadn't worked out. The breakup was for the best. Still, a broken engagement was completely humiliating. She deserved an Oscar for the performance she'd put on for her family and friends—at the very least a Golden Globe was in order.

Only Jack Lombardi, a guy she'd met and befriended in karate class, knew how miserable it had been for her.

Over pasta dinners and plenty of red wine, he'd listened as Piper unburdened herself. Jack had been totally supportive, vacillating between vowing to physically "take care of Gordon" and gently soothing Piper when she wept. He'd kept reciting the same mantra: She was "much too good for him."

The whole experience with Gordon had left Piper vulnerable and wary of getting romantically involved again. The breakup, along with the never-ending struggle to find acting jobs, had led her to give up her Manhattan apartment and move home to her parents' house in Hillwood, New Jersey. She was just taking a break, just regrouping, she told herself. But now she was officially in the ranks of the "bridge and tunnel" crowd.

Awesome.

Making the wedding cake for Glenna Brooks, along with helping to untangle the deadly web of events preceding the wedding, had certainly distracted Piper and made her feel like she was doing something productive. Now she had nothing on the horizon.

Unless she accepted the job from Jillian Abernathy.

THE PARTY GUESTS SURGED CLOSER to the television to watch the Waterford ball descend in Times Square.

"Five, four, three, two, one. Happy New Year!"

Piper felt a hand on her shoulder. She turned and looked up to see Jack's face. The lines at the corners of his brown eyes crinkled as he smiled at her.

"This is going to be a better year, Pipe," he said. "I know it."

He leaned in, took her firmly in his arms, and gave her a long, tender kiss. Piper felt the warmth of his body against hers and found herself responding.

What was she doing? Maybe she did have feelings beyond friendship for Jack, but they had a great relationship that meant the world to her. This was just going to make it messy.

She pulled away gently.

AFTER EVERYONE ELSE HAD GONE, Piper offered to stay and help straighten up.

"Forget it," said Jack as he peeled the paper wrapping from a cupcake and took a bite. He flopped down on the sofa, cleared some glasses and cocktail napkins, put his feet up on the coffee table, and leaned back. "It's too late, and I'm too tired to clean this mess. It can wait till morning." He patted the cushion beside him. "Why don't you sit down?" he suggested.

Piper perched on the arm of a chair across the room. "It was a great party, Jack," she said. "I think everybody had a good time."

"Did *you* have a good time, Pipe?" There was a hopeful tone to Jack's voice.

"Mm-hmm."

She knew he was looking for an indication of how he should proceed. He needed some sort of sign from her to let him know that she wanted to get closer. She answered by changing the subject.

"I wanted to tell you about a job offer I got this afternoon," she said, trying to ignore the expression of disappointment that flashed across Jack's face. She described Jillian Abernathy's Facebook message, the offer to stay at Elysium, and the backstory of the acid attack and the postponed wedding.

"Do you really want to get involved in something like that?" asked Jack. "It sounds like a mess."

"Ever hear of a happy ending?" asked Piper.

"I've heard of 'em, but I haven't seen that many."

"Poor jaded Jack. Are you really all that cynical?"

"Look who's talking," he said, shaking his head. "You won't let yourself even consider the prospect of letting someone in and being happy. If you ask me, that's pretty cynical."

"I don't know what you're talking about, Jack."

"Yes you do, Pipe. I wish you could have seen the fear in your eyes after I kissed you before."

"That's absolutely ridiculous," she protested. "I'm not

afraid of you, Jack. I'm just happy with the way things are between us right now."

"Well, I'm not," said Jack. "So what do we do about that?"

Piper stood up abruptly. "If you really don't want help cleaning up, I'd better get going."

He didn't try to stop her.

CHAPTER

5

GRIDLOCK L.A. AT PARAMOUNT STUDIOS was the West Coast version of New York's Times Square. Except, unlike the original, it wasn't free. Thousands paid a hundred and fifty to two hundred and fifty dollars to party on the studio's Manhattan set. Food and drink flowed as revelers danced and sang with DJs and live bands, welcoming in the New Year. The midnight countdown on the main stage led to wild cheering, falling confetti, and an impressive fireworks show.

Anastasia Fernands knew firsthand. She had covered the event the previous year. She was determined that this was going to be the last time.

She parked her blue Prius in an almost empty lot on Van

Ness. In a little while, the lot would be packed. Anastasia was early. Whenever she could, she preferred to get her bearings before covering a story. She didn't like surprises, though she didn't expect any tonight.

Anastasia looked up into the dark sky and searched for a star. *Please let my wish come true.*

She strolled around the Paramount lot. The buildings on the faux NYC streets were already bathed with red, green, and blue spotlights. A long red carpet was laid out to welcome VIPs, and a giant Ferris wheel waited to lift partiers into the air. Caterers were stocking the food stations. It was all pretty much the same as last year.

Anastasia looked at her watch. The old year was already over on the East Coast, but there were almost three more hours to go in L.A.

She vowed to herself that she was going to take her destiny into her own hands. That was her New Year's resolution. No more waiting around for the powers at the paper to promote her. No more asking for permission to do a story only to have it denied because the topic wasn't sexy enough. No more reporting for the Style section—though in this town more attention was paid to the Style section than to the headlines on the front page.

That wasn't serious journalism.

She had a story that she wanted to cover. She'd been working on it for months, laying the groundwork. Doing the research had been difficult and painstaking, because nobody wanted to talk about the subject. It was a story that would make her editor sit up and pay attention, an investigative piece that Anastasia would be able to look at with pride.

She was using her vacation time and checking into Elysium.

CHAPTER

6

H E TOSSED, TURNED, AND PUNCHED his pillow. Tired as he was, Jack could not fall asleep. He thought about Piper and the way the evening had ended. She was absolutely maddening, but as much as he sometimes wished it were otherwise, he couldn't stop thinking about her.

He didn't know exactly when his feelings for Piper had changed. But he did know that when she'd been in danger last month, he'd been wild with worry. When she ended up all right, he'd been weak with relief. Jack had pictured what life would be like without Piper in it. He didn't like the view.

He couldn't think of any other option but to be patient and hope that she came around to feeling the same way he did. Piper was worth the wait. He wasn't going to call her. The ball was in her court.

Something else was bothering him. He didn't like the idea of her taking the job in L.A. Though she wouldn't be gone long, that business about the acid attack was disturbing. He didn't want Piper to be even remotely associated with danger.

He wished he could keep her under surveillance. Jack was an expert at trailing suspects. But Piper wasn't a terrorist or a criminal being tracked by the FBI. Following her every move would be stalking—weird and just plain wrong.

Resigned to the fact that he wasn't going to be able to sleep, Jack turned on the light, got of bed, and went to the computer. He read up on Jillian Abernathy, the acid attack, and Elysium.

Then he looked up the definition of the word.

ELYSIUM: ANY PLACE OR CONDITION OF IDEAL BLISS OR COMPLETE HAPPINESS. PARADISE.

Good name for a spa, he thought. Then he read the second definition.

IN GREEK MYTHOLOGY, A PLACE ASSIGNED TO VIRTU-OUS PEOPLE AFTER DEATH.

CHAPTER

7

PIPER LET HERSELF INTO THE house and quietly made her way to her bedroom. The small night-light glowed in the upstairs hallway. A board creaked as Piper tiptoed forward. Emmett was sleeping on the floor in front of her parents' room. He lifted his head from his paws, saw it was Piper, and then closed his eyes again.

As she undressed, Piper continued to replay the episode with Jack, keeping up the mental conversation with herself she had had the whole ride home. On the one hand, she was happy that Jack wanted to be with her; on the other, she was scared to go forward with a deeper, more committed relationship. Why couldn't Jack understand that and give her some space?

Throwing her skirt on the chair, Piper decided: She could give herself the space. She was going to agree to make the wedding cake for Jillian Abernathy. The time away might give her some perspective.

Breathing room.

CHAPTER

8

*W*HAT IS THE WORLD COMING *to? Aren't there any manners left? Sending an invitation like this in an e-mail?*

DR. VERNON ABERNATHY AND IRENE WALLACE ABERNATHY

REQUEST THE PLEASURE OF YOUR COMPANY

AT THE MARRIAGE OF THEIR DAUGHTER

JILLIAN MARIE

TO

DR. BENJAMIN DIXON

AT THE GAZEBO AT ELYSIUM

ON SATURDAY THE FIFTEENTH OF JANUARY

AT FOUR O'CLOCK IN THE AFTERNOON

AND AFTERWARD AT

THE RECEPTION.

An electronic wedding invitation was offensive. But the ceremony was just two weeks away. Not really enough time to send out engraved invitations and wait for the response cards.

Unfortunately, the acid missed its mark, but it was good that Jillian had canceled the wedding. It was a victory of sorts. Knowing that Jillian's life had been turned upside down was satisfying.

But obviously the wedding hasn't been canceled. Only postponed.

That poor Flores woman is scarred for life, and Jillian is carrying on with hers.

It isn't right.

CHAPTER

9

New Year's Day . . . Fourteen Days Until the Wedding

I T WAS STILL DARK OUTSIDE.

Other people got to sleep late, lounge around in bed, and have the day off. Hudson Sherwood reached out to silence the alarm, sighing deeply and remembering the time when he was one of those people. No more.

Now holidays were just workdays. The Hollywood Haven Hotel was open seven days a week, three hundred and sixty-five days a year. Somebody had to staff the reception desk. Hudson got stuck with it most weekends.

Once, when he had complained, the hotel manager had shrugged, indifferent and unsympathetic. If Hudson didn't like the way things were, he could try to get a job elsewhere. The manager knew that it would be easy to get another desk clerk. There were lots more people looking for jobs than there were available positions.

Hudson didn't complain again.

As he showered, he thought about his days at Elysium. The spa had also been open year-round, but that hadn't kept Hudson from being free on every single holiday. After all, he was the director. It was the staff, the underlings, who had to work on the holidays. Not Hudson.

Those were the days when he actually had things to do on the holidays. He would fly back east to visit his elderly mother. Or, if he stayed in Los Angeles, there were dinners and parties to attend. Once he lost his position at Elysium, he found that the invitations dried up. He came to realize that the people he'd thought were friends weren't bothering with him anymore. They had included him because of what he did rather than who he was.

He turned off the water and grabbed a towel. After drying himself, Hudson wiped the steam from the bathroom mirror. As he shaved, he almost didn't recognize himself. His sharp features were even more pronounced because of the weight he'd lost. His complexion was pasty. His graying hair was receding more every day.

He dressed quickly, wincing as he always did when he put on the hotel jacket. A stiff uniform was fine for somebody else, but not for him. Considering his past, it was another indignity to be suffered.

Going to the kitchen, Hudson poured a bowl of Raisin Bran. He took it to the living room and sat on the sofa. He looked around the apartment. When he purchased it, he had still been working at Elysium. The furnishings reflected that. Nothing but the best. Now some of the upholstered pieces were faded and frayed, and the rooms could use a fresh coat of paint, but basically the place looked pretty good. He loved his apartment. He prayed all the time that he wouldn't have to sell it.

He worried about it constantly. He had gone through all his savings. After his mother died, Hudson discovered she'd taken a reverse mortgage on her house, which left only a few thousand dollars' inheritance. That money, too, went quickly.

His credit cards were maxed out, and he was friendless and embarrassed about how far he'd fallen. He didn't belong in Los Angeles anymore. He wasn't beautiful enough or young enough or connected enough.

Losing his position at Elysium had started the downward spiral. For a while he'd found work at a less prestigious spa, but he hadn't been able to conceal his contempt for the place. After a few months, he was fired. The next spa he worked at was even worse.

When he lost that position, Hudson decided to try fine hotels. But his anger and resentment sabotaged any success and led to still more dismissals.

Each successive job was another step downward. And for that there was only one person to blame.

CHAPTER

10

THE FIRM KNOCK ON THE bedroom door was followed by her mother's call from the hallway. "You better get up, Piper. Robert and Zara are coming for brunch at noon."

Piper rolled over and moaned. What a way to start the new year. Zara was her sister-in-law, but she was also one of Piper's least favorite people. The idea of spending the afternoon with her was unappealing at best, nauseating at worst.

What did Robert see in that woman? Piper would feel sorry for her older brother if he didn't seem so inexplicably pleased with his wife. Whatever. Who was *she* to decide what made a relationship work? She couldn't get one right herself.

Piper reached over and grabbed her BlackBerry from the bedside table. Checking it, she found she had no missed calls or new voice messages. Jack hadn't called.

She sighed. *He'll call eventually, right?*

Determined not to analyze the events of the night before, Piper logged onto Facebook and updated her status.

SO I'M THINKING A LITTLE WORKING VACAY IS THE PERFECT WAY TO START THE NEW YEAR!

IDEAS?

FRESHLY SHOWERED AND DRESSED IN a red Urban Outfitters sweater and black leggings, Piper bounded down the short staircase that led from the bedrooms to the living area of the house. Her parents were in the kitchen. Vin was having a cup of coffee with the newspaper spread out before him on the table. Terri was washing and slicing fruit at the sink. Platters of crumb cake and bagels were on the counter, along with a French-toast casserole ready to be put into the oven.

Piper gave both her parents kisses. "Happy New Year," she said, picking off a piece of crumb cake.

"You, too, sweetheart," said Terri, followed by a cry as she pulled up the knife. "Oh, great. I just cut myself."

Piper felt a catch in her throat. The news that her mother had macular degeneration was relatively fresh. Cutting a finger was an accident anyone could have. It was a common thing. But now Piper automatically thought it was because of her mother's failing eyesight.

"Here, Mom. Let me." Piper stood next to her mother, gently nudging her aside.

"I can do it," said Terri. "Don't baby me, Piper. I'm warning you."

"I know you can," said Piper. "But I want to help. You do something else."

"Everything's pretty much done," said Terri, handing the knife to her daughter. "I'm going upstairs for a Band-Aid."

Piper finished trimming the strawberries and washed a pint of blueberries, combining them in a glass bowl. Then she cut a melon into bite-size cubes.

"The crown prince and his fair maiden are late," she observed, glancing at the wall clock. "Can't they ever come on time?"

Vin shrugged, still engrossed in the newspaper. "What can I tell you?"

"It's just rude," said Piper.

"Forget it, lovey. Don't get the year off on the wrong foot."

"A little too late for that."

Vin looked up. "What's wrong?"

While Piper actually wanted to talk about what had happened with Jack, she knew it was better not to bring her father into it. Vin wasn't exactly impartial when it came to his daughter. There was a definite chance he'd find a way to hold Jack accountable if Vin thought Jack had hurt his little girl.

But in reality it was she who'd done the hurting.

"Nothing," said Piper as the doorbell rang.

Before they even sat down to eat, Robert blurted it out.

"Zara and I are having a baby."

The room filled with a roar of celebration. The grin on her brother's face was contagious. Piper beamed as her parents, and then she, hugged and kissed Robert and Zara. Her sister-in-law smiled wanly, her face colorless.

"That's the most wonderful news!" cried Terri. "When?"

"August," Robert said with pride.

Piper did the mental math. Wasn't there something about waiting till a pregnancy was three months along before telling people? The baby's conception had barely happened. Leave it to her brother to jump the gun.

"I'm going to be a grandmother!" Terri squealed with delight. She turned to her husband and hugged him. "And you're going to be a grandpa."

Piper watched her father's face. She could almost see his mental wheels spinning, calculating what could go wrong and what kind of precautions would have to taken to ensure that his grandchild was safe. Her mother often recounted how thorough her father had been when Robert and Piper were little, how he would lie awake at night after completing his police shift, worrying—not about the thugs and criminals he dealt with on the streets of New York City but about the safety of his children.

Vin went beyond taking merely the standard precautions in the Donovan household, like making sure electrical outlets were covered and chemical-filled household products were stashed well out of reach. He constantly read and researched, determined that his children would be buckled into the best car seats, smeared with the best sunscreen, fed the most nutritious baby food. He was always on the watch for alerts about recalled products. He routinely checked all their toys to make sure none was broken or had pieces that could be choking hazards. He also made sure that the thermostat on the heater was set so that water could never get hot enough to scald. He insisted that Terri start the kids in swimming lessons before they were even walking.

Besides the standard ipecac, calamine lotion, Bactine, and Pedialyte, the medicine cabinet was stocked with first-aid manuals, burn pads, antiseptic wipes, every manner of adhesive bandage, microshields, cold packs, hot packs, latex gloves, and, even though neither child had any allergies, EpiPens, which he also insisted be available in the glove compartment of both family cars. Piper could still remember that every year, along with getting new shoes and school supplies, she would also get a new emergency kit that her father would make up for her to carry in her book bag. He would go over the contents of the kit with her, explaining the use of each item. Sometimes Piper had been frightened at the things her father told her, but he always reassured her.

"Almost everything can be made all right, lovey. The main thing is to be prepared."

Relatives and friends shook their heads and laughed at

Vin's obsession with emergency preparedness. Vin Donovan couldn't have cared less about what they thought. The most important thing to him was the safety of his family.

Piper knew that her father was going to be less than thrilled when she told him she was definitely going out to Los Angeles to make a wedding cake for a bride whom somebody had tried to kill.

AFTER THE PROUD PARENTS-TO-BE LEFT, Piper and her father cleaned up while Terri began making telephone calls to share the exciting news that she was going to be a grandmother. When the last dish was put away, Piper went up to her room. She looked at the clock, calculated that it was noon on the West Coast, and decided it wasn't too early to call Jillian Abernathy.

The phone was answered after the second ring.

"Hello?"

"Hi. Is this Jillian?"

"Yes?" The voice sounded wary.

"This is Piper Donovan. You sent me a message about making your wedding cake."

"Oh, Piper." The voice sounded relieved. "It's great to hear from you. Happy New Year!"

"Thanks. Same to you," said Piper. "It looks like you're really starting it off in a big way."

Jillian laughed. "Ah, yes, the wedding. I hope you're calling to tell me you'll make our cake."

"Actually, I have a few questions," said Piper.

"Sure. What are they?"

"How many people are you having?" Piper asked.

"I'm not exactly sure yet, but definitely less than a hundred. Ben and I don't want a huge wedding. We want it to be a relatively quiet affair. "

"Oh, that's good," said Piper, "because I know I can make a cake that will be big enough to serve a hundred. I want to be up front with you. This would be only the second wedding cake I've ever made."

"Well, you wouldn't know it from the looks of the one you did for Glenna Brooks," said Jillian. "Hers was amazing. My stepmother wants us to use one of the well-known bakeries out here, but I'd so much rather have you."

"Oh. Well, thank you," said Piper. "Did you have anything particular in mind for yours?"

"I'm pretty open-minded about how it would be decorated," said Jillian. "But there is a flavor we'd like. We want a pumpkin cake."

"Wow, that's original!" said Piper as her mind raced. Her mother had a fantastic recipe for pumpkin cake.

"Actually, Piper, I was wondering if you would be willing to let someone else make the cake itself and you put it together and decorate it."

"I don't understand," said Piper.

"Well, my sister is a nun, and her convent supports itself

by selling pumpkin bread made in their kitchen. It would mean a great deal to us to include the convent in our wedding in some way, though none of the nuns will be able to attend, since they're cloistered. They *are* willing to make the cake for us. We think the publicity they could get from this might bring more attention to their pumpkin-bread business."

"Sorry, I'm a little confused," said Piper. "I thought you wanted a quiet wedding—that you didn't want attention."

"That's right," said Jillian. "I don't. But I'm sure we're going to get it anyway."

CHAPTER

11

NEW YEAR'S DAY OR NOT, Irene Wallace Abernathy was with her personal trainer, stretching, twisting, and lifting weights. She was willing to pay extra for the holiday session. She thrived on Jake's unflagging attention and the way he flirted with her. Jake made her feel desirable.

At forty-six, Irene was keenly aware that men didn't look at her the way they once had. There was a time when she dreaded passing a construction site, bracing herself for the whistles and catcalls that always ensued. Now the workmen didn't even look up from what they were doing.

It wasn't that she wasn't attractive. She knew she was. She still had a trim figure, and her face, thanks to the wonders of Elysium, was almost unlined. Irene had taken very good care of herself over the years, making use of the steep employee discount for all her treatments and classes. Now, as Mrs. Vernon Abernathy, she paid nothing.

Still, time and gravity had changed things. It was a constant battle against crepey skin and sagging sinew.

As she panted through her stomach crunches on the floor of the expansive great room, Irene heard the phone ring.

"Do you want to answer that?" asked Jake, his arms rippling with muscles as he held her feet to the floor.

"No, Vernon will get it," she said, pushing a strand of ash-blond hair from her brow.

It was nice having Vernon home today. There were no surgeries scheduled, and he'd promised they would have the day together, just the two of them. They were going to play some golf this afternoon. Irene hoped that the phone call didn't mean he was needed at Elysium. There was always something. Vernon had finally sold his house in Beverly Hills, where he'd lived with his first wife, Caryn, and built the place they lived in now. The new place was on the periphery of the Elysium property, so he would be right there when needed.

Irene winced as she heard her husband's booming voice.

"Jillian, darling. Happy New Year!" Irene couldn't help but notice the enthusiasm and joy in his tone.

There was no getting around it. More than his cosmetic-surgery practice, more than Elysium, more than their marriage, Vernon's relationship with his daughters was most precious to him. It was exceedingly fortunate that his older daughter, Nina, was in a cloister and wasn't able to pop in or call all the time. But Jillian was always in their lives, taking Vernon's attention away.

While she understood that it was natural that Vernon doted on Jillian, Irene thought their lives were too intertwined. Jillian was a grown woman, after all. Vernon didn't have to rush to make things better every time she stubbed her toe.

If this wedding ever happened, perhaps Ben would be able to weaken the excessive father-daughter bond. But Irene wasn't counting on that.

It was frustrating not being number one in Vernon's life, but she was doing all she could to earn that spot. Vernon would see how affectionate and supportive she was as she helped Jillian prepare for the wedding. He would always remember that Irene loved Jillian as if she were her own daughter. That would strengthen Irene's own bond with him.

CHAPTER

12

WEDNESDAY, JANUARY 5 . . . TEN DAYS UNTIL THE WEDDING

THE TREATMENT ROOM WAS SPARKLING clean and outfitted with sterilized equipment and instruments. Shelves of glass-fronted cabinets on the walls held bottles and jars of various serums, lotions, and tonics designed to correct a wide range of skin conditions, improve appearance, and turn back the hands of time. Chemical peels to reduce fine lines and age spots, depilatory wax to remove unwanted facial hair, serums to cleanse pores and improve skin tone.

Wearing his immaculate lab coat, Kyle Quigley was organizing the gauze, cream, and utensils needed for his next appointment when Esperanza arrived.

"You're early today." He smiled as he glanced at the clock on the wall.

"Is it all right?" asked Esperanza.

"Actually, it works out well," said Kyle. "We'll have a little extra time together."

He could read the pleasure in Esperanza's eyes. Kyle knew she had a thing for him, and he didn't see any harm in playing along. It wasn't uncommon for the women and men who came to him for treatment to grow emotionally attached. As they lay on the treatment table, they were so vulnerable. He took care of them and paid attention to them in very personal ways as he spoke to them soothingly and his fingers caressed their skin. They felt he was on their side, helping them and committed to their health and well-being. They responded to that, often confiding in him. More than one had wanted to have a relationship outside the treatment room and off Elysium's grounds.

Of course, Esperanza had been disfigured, but even if she hadn't been, she wasn't the kind of woman he found attractive. Kyle watched as she climbed onto the table, lay back, and comfortably settled herself. He took off her mask gently. He was careful not to show any emotion as he looked at her face. If Esperanza were to detect any distaste in his expression, she would be traumatized. Poor thing. When she returned to the real world, she was going to suffer horribly at the revulsion in people's eyes when they saw her.

He adjusted the magnifying glass and inspected the dreadfully damaged skin.

"You continue to heal nicely, Esperanza."

"Really?" There was hope in her voice. "I don't look in the mirror."

That's probably just as well, thought Kyle. *But sooner or later you're going to have to see yourself. And when you look in that mirror, you're going to be crushed.*

As Kyle put on the peach-colored latex gloves, he didn't notice Esperanza's expression change.

He painstakingly applied the cream designed to prevent and reduce scars as Esperanza's eyes searched his face. Kyle was careful to make sure that his own expression remained benign, betraying no reaction to what remained of Esperanza's skin. That was the professional thing to do.

He had trained long and hard to become a paramedical aesthetician. Not only could he do cosmetic treatments at Elysium, he could work with dermatologists and plastic surgeons. His ministrations prepared the skin for surgery and a more comfortable healing process. He could offer services that would normally be available only through a medical doctor. Dr. Abernathy trusted him and relied on him. Kyle was exceedingly proud of that.

"Okay," he said, stepping away from the table and pulling off his gloves. "All done."

Esperanza sat up. "Dr. Abernathy tells me I can leave here in a few days," she said, staring down at her lap. "I don't want to go. I like it here. Everyone takes such good care of me." She looked up at Kyle. "*You* take such good care of me."

Here we go, thought Kyle. *Say something reassuring, but don't lead her on, don't hurt her.*

"It's wonderful that Dr. Abernathy thinks you've healed enough to go home, Esperanza. And don't worry. We'll still be seeing each other. You'll be coming back for outpatient visits, won't you?"

She nodded. "But it's not only leaving here that worries me. I'm afraid."

"Of what?"

"That the devil with the acid will come and find me." Her voice trembled.

Kyle reached out and covered her hand with his. "Have you heard anything more about the police investigation?" he asked.

"No, not in weeks and weeks. The detective told me that they are still looking but need more to go on."

"They'll find him," said Kyle, with more conviction in his voice than he actually felt.

Tears welled up in Esperanza's eyes. "I think I could help the police," she said.

"What do you mean?"

"I remember something from that day. Something I didn't remember before."

"What?" asked Kyle. "What do you remember?"

But Esperanza shook her head and kept silent.

CHAPTER

13

A FTER DINNER PIPER FINISHED PACKING. She was excited to be getting away from the biting cold in the Northeast. A visit to the Internet had informed her that January was the coldest month of the year in Los Angeles, with temperatures in the sixties during the day and the forties and fifties at night. What a perfect climate!

Along with black pants, jeans, leggings, tops, yoga clothes, two dresses, a cotton sweater, a bathing suit, and a crushable straw hat, Piper placed a securely wrapped package in the suitcase. The parcel contained tracing paper and the piping tips, pastry bags, flower nails, and other tools she would need to fashion blossoms, stars, leaves, hearts, or whatever else ended up decorating the wedding cake.

As she was selecting the toiletries she wanted to take with her, there was a knock at her bedroom door.

"Come in," she called.

Terri walked into the room with her arm outstretched. "Here," she said, holding out two index cards. "This is my recipe for cream-cheese icing. In my opinion that's the best frosting for pumpkin cake. And the other is the recipe for the pumpkin cake we make at the bakery, just in case you need it."

"Thanks, Mom. I appreciate that."

Piper looked at the cards. She was well aware of the years and effort her mother had put into perfecting every recipe. Terri Donovan's hard work had made The Icing on the Cupcake a resounding success. Piper was the beneficiary, her mother eagerly and generously passing on her priceless expertise.

"You know, Mom, we should really put together all your recipes and make a cookbook or something."

"Maybe one of these days," said Terri as she sat on the edge of the bed.

"I know what that means," said Piper. "That means you have no intention of doing it."

Terri smiled. "Probably not." She cocked her head and squinted as she perused the open suitcase. "Got everything you need?"

"I think so," answered Piper. "If I've forgotten anything, I can buy it out there."

"Just be careful, will you?" Terri took hold of her daughter's arm.

"I will," said Piper, picking up Terri's hand and kissing it. "I know you and Dad aren't crazy about the idea of my doing this. But I'm sure it's going to be fine. You guys just worry about me way too much. Especially Dad."

"We love you, Piper, and we don't want anything to happen to you. As for your father, he's seen a lot, and he knows that real evil exists in the world. He wants you to be prepared. In fact, he's in the basement right now, putting together a special kit for you to take with you."

"Figures," said Piper, shaking her head.

Mother and daughter looked at each other and smiled.

Before going to bed, Piper went down to see her father. Vin was sitting at his workbench with his back to her. She came up behind him, leaned around, and gave him a kiss on the cheek.

"The car service is coming really early to take me to the airport, Dad. I want to say good-bye now."

Vin looked into her eyes. "You're sure you really want to do this, Piper?"

She nodded firmly. "Mm-hmm. For all the reasons we've already gone over."

Vin let out a deep sigh. "All right, then," he said. "I want to go through a few things with you."

"Of course you do."

"Acid is reactive, lovey. When it comes into contact with another material, something is going to happen. If it comes in contact with any part of your body, it will rapidly break down the tissue, causing severe burns. To say it hurts like hell would be an understatement. Shock could set in. And burns can lead to secondary problems, like infection. And infection can lead to—"

"Okay, Dad," said Piper, cutting her father off. "I get it."

"I just want you to understand that burns are never trivial. Not to mention, for an actress, facial burns would very likely end any chance for a career."

"Are you *trying* to scare me?" asked Piper. She wrapped her arms around herself, suddenly chilly.

"If that's what it takes to get you to be careful, then yes." Vin unzipped the compact black nylon bag on his workbench. "Let me show you what's in here."

Piper knew there was no point in protesting that she didn't want to take the bag with her to California. She resigned herself to paying attention as her father emptied its contents.

"Here are safety goggles and a face shield," Vin said, handing the items to her. "Sulfuric acid can erode concrete and etch metal. Imagine what it could do your eyes and face."

"Dad, I'm going to be making a cake. I'm not working with chemicals."

Vin ignored her and continued, taking plastic bottles

from the bag. "If, God forbid, acid does get in your eyes, here is sterile water. Flood your eyes with it, over and over. If you run out of the sterile stuff, use lukewarm water from the tap. And here are tissues, a mirror, and eye patches."

"Really, Dad?" Piper said incredulously. "I'm making a *wedding cake.*"

"And what if you're busy making your cake and somebody comes into the kitchen with his sulfuric acid and a plan to splash it all over you?" Vin didn't wait for an answer to his question. "Here's an acid-resistant apron and gloves. Wear them."

Piper took the apparel from her father.

"Now, if you do come in contact with acid, rapid treatment is essential," said Vin. "You have to get the acid off your body right away. Find a shower or a hose. Start washing while removing your clothes as quickly as you can. To hell with modesty. Strip off everything, even your shoes, and keep the water flowing for at least fifteen minutes. Do not apply any burn ointment or spray."

"Okay, Dad. Okay."

"I've written down all the information, including the hospital emergency room nearest to Elysium. Call 911 right away."

"Man, how did I end up with such a lazy father?" Piper smiled, trying to lessen the tension.

"Oh, yeah, one more thing, lovey. If acid is swallowed, it will burn all the way down to the stomach. It's important not to throw it up, because that will make for additional burning as the acid comes up again."

"So what do I do?"

"Drink milk mixed with egg whites."

"Perfect," said Piper. "I'll mix that right up while the acid is eating through my esophagus."

CHAPTER

14

H UDSON HAD A STANDING CARD game every Wednesday
night. He looked forward to it—not only because he
liked to play gin but because he liked Michael Ghant, the
evening security guard at Elysium, and he wanted to main-
tain their friendship. Hudson Sherwood also liked to keep
up with what was happening at the spa, and the conversation
during their card game provided a weekly update.

At a few minutes before 9:00 P.M., Hudson drove through
the rear entrance to the Elysium property, a small unmarked
driveway off the main road. One hundred yards in, he turned
off the car's headlights. He knew the paved single lane well,
and the glow coming from the windows of Vernon Abernathy's house, set back from the road, provided some illumi-

nation. Hudson silently seethed, as he always did, when he coasted by the gorgeous home.

Dr. Abernathy had done him wrong. There he was in a sprawling, luxurious mansion, with a second wife who was almost as attractive as his first one. Meanwhile Hudson was barely making his monthly bills, racking up debt, and working as a lowly desk clerk in a second-rate hotel for a boss he couldn't stand. Where was the justice in that?

Hudson parked his car farther down the private road, in a small clearing behind some tall bamboo plants. He got out, watchful to avoid any guests or staffers who might be outside enjoying some night air. Hudson quickly walked the rest of the way to the guardhouse. Michael was waiting there for him.

They played a couple of hands. Hudson drank one of the beers he'd brought with him. Michael didn't. He never did.

"I hope Vernon Abernathy and that daughter of his appreciate what they have in you, Michael. You are such a straight arrow."

Michael smiled. "Not that straight. I don't think Dr. Abernathy would appreciate the fact that I have you here to play cards every week."

"True," said Hudson. "You've been loyal, buddy, and I appreciate it. Whenever I bump into anybody else from Elysium, they can't wait to get away from me."

Michael shrugged as he shuffled the deck. "You hired me—of course I'm loyal to you. But try not to take it personally. It's not that they don't like you, Hudson. You were pretty popular when you worked here. They're just uncomfortable, knowing how you were treated and all."

"I get it," said Hudson, nodding. "Their allegiance lies with the hands that feed them. Vernon's and Jillian's."

"Cut," Michael instructed, tapping his index finger on the deck.

Hudson did as he was told. He waited for the cards to be dealt.

"How *is* Jillian doing anyway?" Hudson asked. "I heard she's finally going ahead with the wedding."

"Yeah, it's on for a week from Saturday," said Michael as he picked up his cards and fanned them. "But who knows? I heard something today that might bring up all that nastiness from last year and could knock Jillian for a loop again."

Hudson looked up from his cards. "What?"

"The woman who took the acid in her face?"

"Yeah?" Hudson leaned closer. "She's been staying here at Elysium, right?"

"Right," said Michael as he slapped down the queen of spades. "All this time she hasn't been able to recall much about the attack or her attacker. I heard today that she's finally remembered something."

CHAPTER

15

*T*HE WORD IS OUT. DESPITE *the extreme confidentiality that is supposed to characterize Elysium, people's private information is discussed all the time. The staff thrives on being "in the know." Workers eagerly and magnanimously contribute to the Elysium grapevine whatever information they pick up.*

Sometimes the whispers are about which actor or actress has checked in and what work he or she is having done. Sometimes the whispers are about the way a star has let herself deteriorate or the fact that she's been caught with cocaine. Sometimes the whispers report the details of an intensely personal conversation overheard between a husband and a wife, a parent and a child, an actor and an agent.

Today the whispers were about Esperanza Flores and the

news that she's beginning to have memories of the acid attack. Memories that Esperanza has been unable to tell the police, because up till now her mind has mercifully blocked them out.

She hasn't gone to the police. Yet. She isn't going to either.

One of the maids overheard her on the phone. From Esperanza's side of the conversation, the maid gleaned that the police were coming to Elysium to interview and take her statement tomorrow.

No way can that be allowed to happen.

It's too bad that it had to come to this. Jillian was the target. Esperanza was an innocent victim. She doesn't deserve all the pain she's been through. She doesn't deserve to die.

But in a way it would be doing the poor girl a favor. If she lives, Esperanza is going to have a very tough life.

Soon she'll be at peace.

CHAPTER

16

THE MINUTE THE PLANE TOUCHED down on the tarmac
at Los Angeles International Airport, Piper switched
on her BlackBerry. She was stoked to see an e-mail message from Gabe about an audition he'd set up for next
week in downtown L.A. Still nothing from Jack. Was it
possible that he was so upset with her that now he actually didn't want to have any kind of relationship with her
at all?

Determined not to wallow in worry, Piper updated her
Facebook page with information she'd been eager to share
since she read it in the airline's magazine.

I'M HERE IN THE GOLDEN STATE!

IT SEEMS CALIFORNIA GOT ITS NAME FROM LEGENDARY QUEEN

CALIFIA, WHO RULED A TRIBE OF AMAZONS IN A LAND RIFE

WITH GOLD. MEN WERE ALLOWED ONLY ONE DAY A YEAR TO

PERPETUATE THE RACE.

HMMM . . .

Arriving in the baggage-claim section, Piper scanned the area. She saw a man in a peach golf shirt holding up a paper sign with DONOVAN written across the front. She smiled as she approached him.

"Hi, I'm Piper Donovan."

"How many bags do you have, miss?" the driver asked.

"Just this one that I was able to fit in the overhead," said Piper, looking down at the wheeled duffel bag. "When I was a kid, I lost a bag and was totally traumatized." She didn't mention that the decision not to check her bag had resulted in the confiscation of the bottles of sterile water and the can of mace her father had insisted she bring.

The driver took the handle of the bag from her and led the way out to the parking lot and a black limousine. Piper got into the back of the car, appreciating the soft leather and eyeing the refreshments offered on the serving tray affixed to the rear of the driver's seat. Perrier, juice, nuts, granola bars, and packets of dried fruit. It didn't get much healthier than that. Too bad what she really wanted was a cheeseburger and fries. Or, better yet, a plate of Jack's carbonara.

She missed him.

CHAPTER

17

J ILLIAN HELD UP HER ARMS as the frothy white wedding gown was slipped over her head. Irene then called in the tailor. While her stepmother watched, Nathaniel fastened the back of the dress.

Holding out the gorgeous ruffled skirt, Jillian looked at herself in the full-length mirror and frowned. "It's just hanging on me," she said.

"You've lost weight over these past months, dear," said Irene, putting her arm around Jillian's shoulders. "But it's much better than gaining. Just think about all the fun you can have trying to put some back on."

Jillian climbed up on the stool that Nathaniel had brought with him. Pulling straight pins from the little cushion strapped to his wrist, he fitted the dress to Jillian's body.

The waist, arms, and bodice were going to require some expert needlework.

"You were so wonderful to do this, Irene," Jillian said. "To have Nathaniel come here to do the fitting saved me from having to go downtown. I appreciate that you're trying to make life easier for me."

"It's my pleasure, dear," said Irene, hugging her. "I know I can't ever fill your mother's shoes, Jillian, but I want to be there for you, in whatever ways I can."

When the pinning was finished, Nathaniel went out into the hall while Jillian carefully took off the dress. Irene put it on the hanger and zipped up the long garment bag. The tailor returned to take the bag from her.

"I'll take the dress down to the shop where we bought it, Nathaniel. They'll do the actual alterations."

After Irene paid the tailor and escorted him to the front door, she went back upstairs. Jillian was already dressed to leave for work.

"Do you have to go to Elysium right away?" asked Irene. "I was hoping you'd have time to look at the photo album I've put together."

The two women sat on the edge of the bed. Jillian flipped quickly through the pages of the album, dutifully making comments on each photo. Irene had gathered pictures from Jillian's babyhood and childhood through to her teenage years and young adulthood. The last picture showed Jillian and Ben at their engagement party, which had been held a month before the acid attack.

"I'll treasure this, Irene," said Jillian, "and I'll definitely look at it again when I have the time to really appreciate it." She closed the book. "But I have to run. Piper Donovan gets here today. I want to be at Elysium to welcome her."

"I totally understand, darling." Irene smiled. "I'll put the album in your hope chest. It will be safe there."

CHAPTER

18

E SPERANZA WAS EXCITED AND NERVOUS. Excited because the spa's best colorist was coming to the cottage to tint her hair. Nervous because the police detective would be coming shortly afterward.

The colorist was Jillian's gift. Esperanza could never have afforded him. She knew that because she had checked the little book in the desk drawer that listed all the services offered at Elysium, along with their prices. Esperanza figured that for the amount of money the Elysium colorist charged, she could dye her hair forty times over with the drugstore brand she usually bought.

Picking up the end of a section of hair, Esperanza looked down at the yellow tips. They were the last vestiges of the color she had used so that she would look more like Jillian. She wondered what would have happened if she hadn't done that. Maybe she wouldn't be scarred forever if she'd been satisfied to be herself.

There was a knock at the cottage door. A man carrying a case entered. He smiled as he held out his hand to Esperanza. But she caught the expression of dismay that flashed across his face as he looked at her.

"I'm Carlo," he said. "Let's play."

They decided that bright blond wasn't the right color for Esperanza. It didn't work with the color of her skin. But she didn't want to go back to the jet-black hair she'd inherited from her parents.

"Caramel," said Carlo. "Not too light, not too dark. A warm, rich caramel color, with just the right highlights, will look wonderful on you."

An hour and a half later, Carlo held up a mirror for Esperanza to inspect her newly colored, shampooed, and conditioned locks.

"What do you think?" he asked, smiling broadly. "Do you like it?"

Esperanza stared at the image in the mirror, struggling to keep her emotions in check. She'd been hoping that it wouldn't be so bad, but her disfigurement was hideous. Her face was distorted, covered in bumps, scars, and mottled skin. She couldn't bear to look at herself.

"It's very nice," she said quietly, averting her eyes.

"Very nice?" Carlo asked incredulously. "It looks terrific! That color is great on you."

"*Muchas gracias,*" Esperanza whispered.

She couldn't wait for him to leave. As soon as Carlo packed up his gear and exited the cottage, Esperanza threw herself on the bed, sobbing.

She was absolutely hideous. Not even the best hair color made would change that. How was she going to be able to face the outside world?

Tears dripped from her eyes. Esperanza tried to catch and wipe them away before they seeped beneath her mask, but some were making it through anyway. She had to stop crying and get ahold of herself.

She rose from the bed and walked into the bathroom. Turning on the tap, she cupped cool water in her hands and slowly rinsed her eyes. She was careful to avoid looking in the mirror over the sink.

She reached for a soft white towel from the rack. As she patted gently at her eyes, she heard a sound from the front of the cottage. The detective must have arrived early. It was time to tell him she remembered the peach-colored gloves.

"I'll be right there," she called. She was folding the towel when the knob on the bathroom door jiggled.

"I said I'll be right there," said Esperanza. "Just take a seat in the living room."

She hung the towel on the rack, smoothed her hair, straightened up, and took a deep breath before opening the door.

CHAPTER

19

PIPER STARED OUT THE WINDOW as the limousine entered the grounds of Elysium. The long driveway was edged with dense trees bearing glossy green leaves and lacy sprays of small white flowers.

"What are those?" she asked.

"Avocado trees," answered the driver. "In a few months, they'll be laden with fruit. We use them in so many things here, from beauty treatments to milk shakes."

The car pulled up in front of a white stucco mansion with a sienna-colored tile roof. A young man dressed in a peach cotton shirt and khaki slacks immediately came to the limousine and opened the rear door.

"Welcome to Elysium, *señorita,*" he said as Piper got out of the car.

She inhaled the sweet, fresh air and looked around. Clusters of palm trees, fronds swaying in the breeze, flanked the mansion. Hibiscus and bougainvillea grew from gigantic clay pots carefully placed around the perimeter of the stone-paved courtyard, while water cascaded over the sides of a three-tiered fountain in the middle. Everything was bathed in Southern California sunlight and exuded a feeling of carefully cultivated well-being.

"Miss Abernathy is expecting you," said the man.

Piper followed as he carried her duffel through the expansive lobby to the massive walnut reception desk at the end of the room. Upholstered chairs were strategically placed near the glass walls that offered breathtaking views of the landscape. The area was quiet, calm, and soothing.

As Piper waited for the desk clerk to complete making notations in the computer, she heard a woman's voice behind her.

"Piper?"

Turning around, she recognized Jillian Abernathy, who was even prettier in person. Piper noticed that the length and color of the woman's hair were almost exactly the same as her own.

The two women shook hands and exchanged greetings.

"That's a long flight," said Jillian. "You're probably beat. There's a masseuse on standby for you. Would you like her to come to your room now?"

"That would be fantastic," said Piper. "Unless you think I should check out the kitchen and tour the rest of the place first."

"It's up to you," said Jillian. "But I usually find that I can pay more attention when I'm rested."

"And I'm in love already," said Piper.

"Good." Jillian turned to the desk clerk. "What room is Miss Donovan in?"

The clerk checked the computer screen as Jillian's phone sounded.

"Excuse me," said Jillian, putting the phone to her ear. She listened, the pleasant expression falling from her face. "Call 911, and I'll be right there," she snapped. Without another word, she took off.

Instinctively, Piper followed.

IT WAS CHAOS IN THE bungalow.

Piper stood to the side of the room and tried to stay out of the way as a man administered CPR to a woman on the floor. A plastic mask hung away from the woman's face, revealing grotesquely ravaged, red skin. In stark contrast was the beautiful caramel-colored hair that fanned out around her head.

"Oh, my God! Dear God, no!" Jillian Abernathy cried, rocking herself. "This can't be happening. It can't be. Please, Esperanza. Live. You've got to live!"

As Piper stared, she began to make connections. The woman who lay crumpled on the floor with wide-open, bloodshot eyes and a dark red trickle oozing from her nose was the same woman who had suffered the acid attack meant for Jillian Abernathy.

Ambulance technicians arrived, and the man who'd been administering CPR moved back and put his arm around Jillian. Piper suddenly recognized him. He was the guy in Jillian's Facebook picture. Her fiancé.

The EMTs applied paddles to Esperanza's chest, but neither the shocks nor the injection of something into the woman's chest produced the desired result.

After Esperanza's body was taken away, Piper was grateful that Elysium was a private facility and that the media were not allowed on the grounds. She wouldn't want her parents, or anyone else for that matter, to see what she had just seen. The only pictures of Esperanza Flores had been taken by the police photographer.

It was a sight that Piper doubted she would ever forget.

CHAPTER

20

IF SHE POSITIONED HERSELF IN just the right way, Wendy could catch a glimpse of Cottage 7 from her window. She had watched people running past her own cottage and had seen a crowd form in front of the other building. Wendy had wanted to go see what was happening, but that was out of the question.

There was no way she would venture out there and show herself to all those people. She couldn't deal with their averted glances and outright stares. Wendy completely understood people's reactions. If *she* couldn't stomach the way she looked, how could they?

In their therapy sessions together, Dr. Ben was trying to help her come to believe that how she looked wasn't the essence of who she was. Dr. Ben said that her appearance was just the outer, less important shell. What was inside—her mind, her feelings, her personality, her spirit—made up the real Wendy. That's what Dr. Ben believed.

Or that was what Dr. Ben *said* anyway. When it came right down to it, Dr. Ben was marrying one of the most gorgeous women Wendy had ever seen. Wendy doubted that he'd been initially attracted to Jillian Abernathy by her mind. Maybe he came to love her after getting to know her better, but he had to want to get to know her in the first place. Initial physical attraction counted. There was no denying that.

Who was ever going to be attracted to a woman with almost no nose?

She was a freak show.

While her father blamed Dr. Abernathy's surgery, Wendy knew she had to take some responsibility. Her own obsession with her appearance had brought her to this place. She hadn't liked the way her nose looked and had badgered her father to pay for fixing it.

Her father had been so resistant. He'd insisted she was beautiful just the way she was. Her nose was unique and made her face the one he had loved since the day she was born. It was as much a part of her as the freckles sprinkled across it, her curly red hair, and her big brown eyes. But Wendy kept at him and kept at him until she wore her father down. She convinced him that she hated her nose so much that she could never even begin to be happy until it was changed. And ever since Wendy's mother had deserted them years ago, her father was desperate to make his daughter happy.

She hadn't been satisfied with the results of the first surgery. The second surgery only made it worse. When the bandages were taken off after the third surgery, there was very little cartilage left.

Her father said it was a nightmare and that Dr. Abernathy would have to pay. He had talked to an attorney about it. But Dr. Abernathy was trying to stave off the lawsuit. Wendy could stay at Elysium free of charge while she recuperated and Dr. Abernathy tried to figure out how to proceed with further corrective surgery. In the meantime she was in therapy with Dr. Ben to help her cope.

She would give anything to look the way she once had.

Wendy was diverted from her thoughts by the knock on the cottage door.

"Who is it?"

The door opened.

"It's me." Her father poked his head in and smiled at her. Wendy knew his smile was forced.

"You're early today," said Wendy as George Ellis put his key in his pocket and gently kissed his daughter on the cheek.

"Couldn't wait any longer to see my girl. How are you?"

"Okay, I guess," said Wendy. "Something must have happened at Cottage Seven. That's where the woman who worked for Jillian Abernathy and was splashed with acid is staying."

"Yeah, I saw the cops and a couple of EMTs," said George. "Why don't we take a walk over there and see what's going on?"

Wendy adamantly shook her head. "Uh-uh."

"Come on, sweetheart," urged George. "This is a good opportunity to get out for a little while. You don't have to worry about anyone staring at you. They'll all be focused on what's happening at the cottage."

"I said *no*, Dad."

"You know, Wendy, someday you're going to have to face the world, honey," said George as he sat on the bed.

"I know it, Dad. But every time I think about that, I just want to die."

AFTER VISITING WITH HIS DAUGHTER, George walked over to Cottage 7. The crowd had broken up, and the EMTs were gone, yet there were still two policemen outside. Yellow tape had been stretched across the cottage door and cordoned off the area around the little house.

George noticed a woman with short dark hair leaning against a palm tree. She was wearing one of Elysium's peach treatment smocks, so he surmised she was a guest. The woman was holding her hand up to her mouth as her eyes remained trained on the cottage. She didn't notice as George approached, and she was startled when he cleared his throat.

"Excuse me," he said.

The woman's head turned quickly to look at him, and

the hand near her mouth dropped. Before she could shove her hand into her pocket, George saw that it held what looked like a small electronic device. A phone? A recorder?

"Do you know what happened?" he asked.

The woman nodded toward the cottage. "The woman who was staying there was found dead."

"The girl who'd been attacked with acid?" asked George.

"Yes, I think so," said the woman.

George felt sorry for the young woman who'd been killed. The poor thing had suffered terribly from her association with the Abernathys—just as he and his daughter had. But he didn't feel one bit bad about the negative publicity that would inevitably be generated by the death. Anything that hurt Elysium, and therefore Vernon Abernathy, was fine as far as George was concerned.

CHAPTER

21

THE SCENE AT COTTAGE 7 had left Piper shaken and tense.
That poor woman—living through the agony of the
acid attack and the months of pain that followed was more
than anyone should be forced to experience. And now . . . to
be brutally murdered.

It was also extremely unnerving to realize that a killer
had struck—in the middle of the day, and so close by. Piper
shuddered involuntarily.

When she finally reached her room, she felt relief as she
viewed the space she would be living in for the next few
days. Rather than a single bedroom, Jillian had arranged for
a suite. The living room was decorated in Spanish Colonial
style, with natural-linen-upholstered furniture and a large,
multicolored handwoven rug. A desk held a two-line phone

as well as a directory of spa services, menus, and an explanation of how to access the high-speed Internet. There was a fireplace in the corner, a flat-screen television mounted on the wall, and sliding glass doors that opened onto a private balcony offering a view of Los Angeles below.

A four-poster king-size bed, appointed with luxurious white linens, dominated the adjoining room. Piper noticed that her bag already rested on the luggage rack. A fresh copy of the *Los Angeles Times* lay folded on the bedside table. Peach-colored slippers embroidered with the Elysium emblem were lined up on the floor next to the bed.

Walking into the bathroom, Piper let out a little "Yay!" A sunken tub lined with Mexican tiles was situated next to a picture window affording a spectacular vista of the hills and sky. An assortment of soaps, salts, shampoos, lotions, and creams, as well as stacks of soft towels, sat on the shelves. Two plush terry-cloth robes hung from hooks on the wall. White candles perched on a dozen wrought-iron holders were carefully placed around the room.

Piper considered taking a long, hot bath, but she knew that would just lead her to crawl into the big bed and take a long nap. After seeing what had happened to Esperanza Flores, Piper didn't feel like being alone. She was eager to explore Elysium, starting with the swimming pool.

THOUGH THE OUTDOOR POOL AT Elysium was heated, the air temperature was a little too cool for Piper to get excited about actually going into the water. She was content to find an empty lounge chair. She selected a shady spot that faced the pool but backed up to a hedge of bamboo and giant fern-like plants.

Within a minute or two of her settling down on the peach-canvas-covered lounge cushion, a young man in an Elysium shirt asked Piper if she would like a drink.

"I'll have an iced tea," she said. "And can you put some lemonade in that?"

"You mean an Arnold Palmer?" asked the waiter.

Piper nodded. "Sounds great."

"Anything else?"

She suddenly realized she hadn't had anything to eat since the bag of Munchies snack mix on the plane. She looked at her watch and realized that dinner was a couple of hours away, so she ordered a blueberry muffin to tide her over.

As she waited, Piper surveyed the pool area. At the entryway a small shed held towels for the guests. There were about two dozen lounge chairs arranged to make sure guests did not feel crowded. A few tables surrounded with straight-backed chairs dotted the stone patio. A man working on a computer sat at one of them. Piper wasn't entirely sure, but the guy looked like one of the older actors from *Ocean's Eleven*, *Twelve*, and *Thirteen*.

There were also separate little areas set off the main patio, offering more privacy for extreme sunbathers, lovers, or guests who just wanted to be alone. When she heard a woman's voice coming from the other side of the hedge, Piper realized that one of the private areas was right behind her.

She caught snatches of what the woman was saying, surmising that she was having a phone conversation, since Piper heard no other voice.

"Couldn't have picked a better time to come here."

"Amazing pictures."

"Even better than I thought."

"Exclusive."

"I'm working on it now and should have it ready in about an hour."

Then no sound came from the other side of the bamboo and ferns.

The waiter brought Piper's order. She sipped her drink and ate half the muffin before her curiosity got the better of her. She got up from her lounge and peeked around the corner of the hedge. The woman she saw had short dark hair and looked to be in her early thirties. There was a wire coming out of her ear, and she was engrossed in what she was typing on her laptop computer.

Piper felt her cheeks flush as the woman looked up and stared straight at her.

"Oh, excuse me," said Piper, flustered.

The woman smiled as she took out her earpiece. "There's nothing to be excused for."

"I didn't want you to think I was spying on you or anything," Piper explained.

The woman laughed. "Don't worry. I can't help myself either—I've got to see who I can recognize. As a matter a fact, there was a movie star down here at the pool a while ago who hasn't done anything in so long that I thought she was out of the business. I gather she's come to Elysium for a little '*freshening.*'"

"Who was it?" asked Piper.

The woman smiled slyly. "That's for me to know and you to find out—if I decide you can be trusted."

"Fair enough," said Piper, returning the smile. She reached out to shake the woman's hand. "I'm Piper Donovan."

"Hi, Piper. I'm Anastasia." She waved to a chair. "Would you like to sit down?"

"Sure." As she took a seat, Piper noticed the tiny recorder with the wire coming out of it sitting on the table next to the computer.

Anastasia studied Piper's face. "Let me guess," she said. "You're an actress."

Piper nodded.

"You're not old enough for a face-lift, and you certainly don't need a tummy tuck or Botox, though Lord knows kids are pumping the stuff into themselves earlier and earlier. Come for some beauty treatments?"

"No," said Piper. "Though I hope to have some while I'm here. Actually, I came to make a wedding cake."

"Really?" Anastasia appeared very interested. "Who's getting married?"

"Jillian Abernathy, the director of this place," said Piper.

"Oh, that's right," said Anastasia, nodding. "I had heard that."

"I just met Jillian a few hours ago. She seems like such a nice person, but I feel sorry for her," Piper said, shaking her head. "Talk about bad karma. First she cancels her wedding after the woman who worked for her took an acid attack meant for Jillian. Now, just as Jillian finally gets it together to go ahead with the wedding, the woman is murdered."

"Yeah, I heard that the woman in Cottage Seven was dead," said Anastasia, "but how do you know it was a murder?"

"I was in the cottage, and before they pushed me out, I heard one of the police talking about her being smothered. It looked like she'd put up quite a struggle." Piper shivered. "I guess they'll do an autopsy to be sure."

"Nice way to start your stay at Elysium," Anastasia murmured, looking at her laptop.

"I'm not going to complain," Piper answered. "I'm still here."

She was sensing that the woman was distracted and ready to wrap up the conversation. It was just as well, thought Piper, feeling the sun beating down on her skin. She was eager to escape its burning rays.

"Well, I guess I'll be seeing you around," she said as she stood.

"Yeah, great, Piper," said Anastasia. "I'm going to be here through next week. I'm sure we'll bump into each other."

Piper walked away, turning to look back as she rounded the hedge. Anastasia was already typing again.

CHAPTER

22

O F ALL THE TASKS SISTER Mary Noelle was assigned, working at the small gift shop of the Monastery of the Angels was her favorite job. She enjoyed stocking the shelves and arranging the items for sale. Prayer cards, religious pamphlets, rosary beads, and hand-crocheted hats, scarves, and afghans sold modestly. Fudge, caramels, peanut brittle, and mints hand-dipped in chocolate sold better. But the biggest seller was the pumpkin bread.

Like the candy, the moist and fragrant pumpkin bread was made by the nuns. Its popularity grew with each new person who ate a piece. Many thought it was hands down the best pumpkin bread they'd ever tasted. Proceeds from the sales were applied to the operating budget of the economically struggling convent.

Sister Mary Noelle felt her stomach rumble. It had been a busy day, and she hadn't eaten lunch. As an extern sister, she was permitted to leave the grounds. One of her responsibilities in the cloistered community was to interact with the outside world. While the cloistered nuns worked inside the convent and concentrated on a contemplative lifestyle, an extern performed the tasks that couldn't be done within the convent's walls: grocery shopping, taking the elderly sisters for medical appointments and tests, buying supplies the convent needed, and doing whatever errands Mother Prioress directed.

This morning Sister Mary Noelle had taken elderly Sister Aloysius to the podiatrist and then to the store to buy special shoes for her arthritic feet. Then she'd taken a shipment of pumpkin bread to FedEx and gone to buy paint and turpentine for the freshening-up of the infirmary walls. After another stop she hurriedly returned to the convent, in time for the strict hour of silence that followed the noonday meal, the largest meal of the day, which she had missed.

Sister Mary Noelle knew that the light supper she would eat after evening prayer wouldn't nearly satisfy her. She was sorely tempted to open up a bag of pumpkin bread, but she restrained herself. It was good to do without.

The bell rang, signaling that there was a customer waiting. Sister Mary Noelle made her way to the black iron door, unlocked and opened it. A young woman with disheveled blond hair and a very troubled expression on her face stood there.

"Jillian! What are you doing here? What's wrong?"

Jillian leaned forward, threw her arms around her sister, and held on tightly. "The most terrible thing, Nina! Esperanza is dead!"

The nun pulled back and stared into Jillian's eyes. "What?" she asked. "The last time we spoke, you told me that she was improving."

"Somebody killed her, Nina. Esperanza was murdered!"

Sister Mary Noelle made the sign of the cross. "God rest her soul," she whispered.

Jillian buried her face in her sister's white habit and sobbed. "I don't know what to do—or where to turn."

"You've come to the right place, Jillian," Sister Mary Noelle said as she patted her younger sister on the back. "You've come to the right place."

CHAPTER

23

ESPERANZA DIDN'T GO EASILY. SHE *twisted and squirmed and pushed as the pillow was held down on her face. She kicked and scratched and tried to escape, fighting death for what seemed an interminably long time. Finally her arms and legs stilled as her body let out one last shudder.*

The thing that stood out most was the terror in her eyes in those first seconds when she saw the peach gloves. In that instant, Esperanza understood that the person who'd scarred her forever with acid had come for her again.

"Diablo!" she whispered before finding her voice and trying to scream. It was no use. All sound was muffled by the pillow.

If Esperanza hadn't begun to remember, perhaps she could have been spared. But she was remembering and therefore had to be stopped. That's just how it was.

In a way she was better off. In this world who would want to live looking like that?

CHAPTER

24

FRIDAY, JANUARY 7 . . . EIGHT DAYS UNTIL
THE WEDDING

THE SHRILL RING REVERBERATED THROUGH the darkness, abruptly waking Piper from a deep sleep. For a moment she felt unable to move, unsure of where she was. Her eyes found the clock on the table next to the bed. Four-thirty.

What?

Rolling over, she groaned as she fumbled for the receiver. Her mouth barely moved as she spoke.

"Hello?"

"Piper? It's Daddy. Why don't you keep your cell phone on? I had to go through the switchboard, and the woman didn't want to put me through because it was so early out there. I had to tell her it was an emergency."

Piper sat upright and turned on the lamp. She squinted as her eyes adjusted to the bright light. "Is everything all right, Dad? Are you and Mom okay?"

"Your mother and I are fine, Piper. I'm calling about you. I just watched a news report on the murder of that Latina out there, the one who'd been sprayed with acid. And who do I see in one of the scenes? You."

Piper tried to concentrate. It was four-thirty here, so that meant it was seven-thirty on the East Coast. Her father always watched *Good Morning America*. It made sense that the murder of Esperanza Flores would be reported, but pictures? No media were allowed on Elysium's property. Had the crime-scene photos taken by the police been released?

"What did the pictures show, Dad?" she asked.

"Exteriors of the cottage the woman was killed in, the cops milling around outside and cordoning off the area with police tape, the body of the Flores woman being carried away. Then, lo and behold, I see my very own Piper Donovan walking across the screen."

"Walking across the screen?" asked Piper. "You mean the pictures weren't still shots?"

"No, they were video. I don't think they were taken by a professional videographer, though. Whoever was holding the camera was shaking a bit. And the quality was good, but not as good as you usually see on the news."

"Somebody probably recorded everything on an iPhone or a BlackBerry," said Piper.

"I don't care *how* the video was recorded," said Vin. "I care about what it *showed*. And I don't like you being in the middle of a crime scene, Piper. *Especially* not a murder scene. I knew you shouldn't have gone out there."

AFTER LISTENING TO A LITANY of instructions and doing her best to reassure her father that she would be very careful, Piper ended the phone call. She switched off the light and snuggled beneath the light down comforter. As she tried to fall back to sleep, her mind raced.

Someone had taken video of the activity outside Cottage 7. Lately it felt as if anyone could pretend to be Diane Sawyer—a staff member, a guest, even one of the EMTs or police. So many people carried cell phones equipped with still and video cameras. Those handheld devices were capable of transmitting video almost instantly via the Internet to other computers and handhelds.

TV news organizations frequently encouraged viewers to send in video of interesting events encountered in their neighborhoods and as they went about their daily lives. Piper herself had shot video of Emmett playing in the snow after the last storm, sent it to *Eyewitness News,* and had been thrilled when she caught sight of her dog in the package that aired on the five o'clock broadcast. Actually, she hadn't seen the piece as it aired. Her father had, and he'd alerted her. Piper was able to watch it online later.

Turning onto her side, she fluffed the pillows and repositioned them under her head. As she struggled to get comfortable, she thought of the conversation she'd overheard at the pool yesterday afternoon. Anastasia had been talking about amazing pictures. Was she the one who'd provided the video that ended up on *Good Morning America*? Was she a reporter?

As she drifted off to sleep again, Piper decided she was going to get to know Anastasia a little better.

CHAPTER

25

A FTER HE WENT FOR HIS early-morning run, Jack got home, kicked off his running shoes, stripped off his hat, scarf, and gloves, then turned on the television set in the living room. He listened to the audio as he went to the kitchen and poured himself a bowl of cereal and milk. He was taking a spoon from the drawer when he heard Robin Roberts, in the studio in New York City, introduce the story.

"Esperanza Flores, the thirty-one-year-old woman from Los Angeles who police think was attacked with acid in a case of mistaken identity, was found dead in a cottage on the grounds of the ultra-spa Elysium, where she'd been staying while she recuperated from damage done by the attack. Police suspect that the death was a homicide and are wondering if the assailant who disfigured Flores last year returned to kill her."

Jack hurried to get a view of the images on the television screen. His jaw clenched when he saw Piper in front of the bungalow where the woman had just been murdered. He grabbed his cell phone and was about to call her, but then he thought better of it. She would still be asleep.

As he showered and dressed for work, Jack was torn. He hated the idea of Piper in the middle of that mess at Elysium. He wanted to call her.

It had been a week since they'd talked, and that last conversation had been painful. He'd been hoping that Piper would call him. But days had gone by, and she hadn't.

She had to be the one to reach out, right? She knew how he felt, how he wanted go forward with their relationship. It was up to her to let him know that she was ready.

But what if she never was?

Jack didn't handle rejection well. He also didn't want to feel like he was helplessly waiting around.

That's why he had a date tonight.

CHAPTER

26

IRENE GOT OUT OF BED slowly, taking great care not to wake her sleeping husband. Vernon had tossed and turned all night. It was just before dawn when he finally fell asleep.

Irene hadn't slept much either. She couldn't turn off her mind.

She shivered as she pulled on a flowing robe. Quietly closing the bedroom door behind her, she tiptoed down the long hallway to the kitchen. The housekeeper already had a pot of coffee brewing.

Irene poured herself a cup, added a little skim milk, and took a seat at the table. Looking out the glass doors to the patio and the lush grounds beyond, she thought about the night before. She'd been trying to comfort Vernon when Jillian, returning from the convent, had come rushing in, throwing herself into her father's arms. Jillian had sobbed and sobbed, and Vernon had tried to soothe her even as he himself was in anguish. Irene had stood by helplessly, knowing that it was pointless to say or do anything.

Vernon was devastated over the fact that Esperanza had been killed. He'd grown quite fond of the young woman and had made it his goal to restore her appearance as much as humanly possible. He'd been deeply shaken by the idea that the acid that had maimed Esperanza had really been meant for his precious Jillian. Vernon was also profoundly grateful that acid had never touched his daughter's beautiful face. Preparing Esperanza to return to the real world had come to be a top priority for him, a way to make reparations.

Irene suspected that Vernon was motivated as much by professional pride as by humanitarian or spiritual concerns. He liked taking on the cases that other plastic surgeons might shy away from. He enjoyed the challenge. Vernon had a top-rated reputation. The men and women who came to him to appear younger, healthier, and happier got what they paid so handsomely for. Dr. Vernon Abernathy's patients didn't walk away looking overly pulled or stretched or pumped with chemicals. They came away looking like themselves, only better.

There were, of course, the rare exceptions.

Wendy Ellis was one of them. What had happened to that girl's nose was a horror show. Vernon was sick about it and worried that a malpractice suit was in the offing. While he was well insured and could afford to pay damages, a lawsuit would be shattering publicity for himself and Elysium.

Irene tapped her nails on the tabletop, trying to think of what to do next. Last night Jillian's first reaction to the murder was that she wanted to postpone her wedding to Ben yet again. Vernon had persuaded her otherwise.

"We need something positive and life-affirming," he'd said. "Not going ahead with the wedding lets whoever killed Esperanza win."

As she finished her cup of coffee, Irene knew what she was going to do. First she was going to walk over to the spa and get a manicure, and then she was going to make some phone calls to see if there were any funeral arrangements set for Esperanza. It might be a good idea to schedule a little memorial service on the grounds of Elysium. That would serve a few purposes: It would allow the staff to pay their respects to the poor girl, as well as showing the guests that Elysium's management acknowledged that a terrible thing had happened. No one was trying to hide anything.

After Irene organized that, she was going to the cottage where Jillian had stayed last night because she didn't want to spend the night in her own house. Irene would continue helping Jillian in any way she could with the wedding preparations.

Vernon would love her for that.

CHAPTER

27

PIPER SLEPT FITFULLY, FALLING IN and out of disturbing dreams, the horror of what she had witnessed the day before organizing itself in her unconscious mind. When she awoke, she stretched, got out of bed, and, grabbing the remote, clicked on the TV as she walked to the French doors that opened onto the terrace. She drank in the view. The sky was clear and blue, the sun was shining brightly, and a mild breeze caused the palm fronds to wave slightly. Heaven. No trace of the violence that had played out in Cottage 7, only several hundred yards away.

She could hear the reporter on the television playing inside. They'd gotten another foot of snow on the East Coast. While Piper hated the thought of her parents dealing with all that, she was thrilled that she was missing it herself.

Now, *this* was living! January, but no heavy coats, no hats, no gloves, and the only scarves worn were light ones draped for style, not warmth. Maybe she should think about relocating for a while. She loved Manhattan, but she knew there was so much more work to be found out here. Los Angeles was *the* place to be for young actors trying to make it in the entertainment business.

She was excited about the audition for the TV commercial Gabe had arranged for her next week. That was the problem, though: She was always excited. Every prospect unleashed her imagination. She knew that one role could lead to another and another and another. In reality she seldom got the roles. Yet she was always able to move forward. Piper knew that she had to keep putting herself out there. She believed that eventually she would find her way.

Piper reminded herself of the primary reason she was here in California: She had a wedding cake to make. Her plan was to go down for some breakfast, explore Elysium a bit more, and then see about going over to the Monastery of the Angels to sample some of the famous pumpkin bread baked in their kitchen and talk to the sisters about how they were going to adapt the recipe to make pumpkin cake. She wasn't quite sure how that would play out, since the sisters were supposed to talk as little as possible.

She dressed in a loose-fitting shirt, a pair of leggings, and flats. Piper pulled her long hair into a ponytail, applied a little mascara and lip gloss, and was ready to go. As she

THE LOOK OF LOVE

left the room, she clicked off the TV, then grabbed a note-
pad and pencil from the desk and put them into her oversize
purse, making certain that her BlackBerry and wallet were
also inside.

There were several empty tables in the dining room, but
when Piper noticed that there was seating on the patio, she
decided to have breakfast outside. Scanning the menu, she ordered an egg-white omelet with spinach, mushrooms, smoked
mozzarella, and tomatoes. While she sipped a glass of fresh-
squeezed orange juice, she settled into her chair and admired
her surroundings.

The patio looked out over the hills in the distance as well
as the sweeping lawns of the Elysium property. An ornate
gazebo stood in the center of the green expanse. Piper took
the pencil and paper from her purse and began to sketch.
Perhaps the gazebo could serve as a starting point for the
wedding cake's design.

"That's a pretty good likeness. It's nice to know our
wedding-cake maker is so artistic."

Piper looked up to see a tall, good-looking man with
dark hair and a bright smile standing next to her chair. She
recognized him as the man who'd been working in vain to
save Esperanza in the cottage the day before.

"I'm Ben Dixon, the groom," he said. "We didn't for-
mally meet yesterday."

"Piper Donovan." They shook hands.

"May I?" he asked.

"Sure," said Piper as Ben seated himself across the table from her. Immediately, a server with a carafe in hand arrived to take his order.

"Just coffee," Ben said as he watched the steaming liquid being poured. "And a bowl of strawberries, please." He turned to Piper. "Yesterday wasn't exactly the best way to get started, was it?"

"No, not quite," she said. "I can't stop seeing that poor woman's face."

"I know what you mean," said Ben. He picked up his cup and drank. "I've seen people die before, but Esperanza's death is especially upsetting. She had already been through so much."

Piper nodded, aware that he was referring to the acid attack. "Did you know her well?" she asked.

"You could say that. I'm a psychiatrist, and Esperanza had been in therapy with me. She was about to leave Elysium."

Piper sighed. "That must have been rough for her. I know it sounds strange, but she probably felt really safe here. And with everything that happened, I'm sure it was nice for her to feel so taken care of. It must have been terrifying to think about going back into the world with such a badly scarred face."

"Especially this town," said Ben. "Look around you, Piper. This whole place is devoted to making people more beautiful, and business is booming. Beauty is a powerful currency in the City of Angels. Someone who is disfigured, especially as badly as Esperanza was, has a miserable time of it."

The server came with Piper's omelet and the strawberries for Ben.

"So," said Piper, picking up her fork, "have you heard anything from the police? Do they have any idea who would have wanted to kill her?"

Ben shook his head. "We haven't heard anything officially, but we're thinking that it might have been whoever threw that acid in her face the first time around. Apparently, though she never told me about it, Esperanza had been having some memory of the attack return. Unfortunately, the word spread around here that she was going to be talking to the police."

"And the killer found out and silenced her before she could," said Piper.

Ben shrugged. "Maybe."

"I'm sorry," said Piper.

"Of course you are," said Ben.

"Yeah, I am sorry about Esperanza, very sorry," she said. "But I meant I was sorry about all this happening right before your wedding."

"Me, too," said Ben. "Jillian is a wreck. She's afraid to be alone for a minute."

CHAPTER

28

THE VIDEO ON *GOOD MORNING America* and the story in the *Los Angeles Times* were a double punch. Vernon threw the newspaper down, knocking over his glass of orange juice. The liquid spilled onto his lap.

"Damn it!" he yelled, his face reddening beneath his tan.

Irene attempted to soothe her husband. "Vernon, try to relax, dear. Everything will be all right."

Vernon leaned back, ran his fingers through his white hair, and held his head. "No, it will *not* be all right, Irene. People are going to think that Elysium is unsafe. The media are camped out front, blocking the entrance. Look at these pictures. Who's going to want to come to a place where people are murdered? Bad enough that people still bring up Caryn's death, and it's just a matter of time before George Ellis files a malpractice suit against me for what I did to his daughter."

"You weren't responsible for Caryn's death, and everyone knows it. She had a heart attack. And if George Ellis decides to sue, you'll probably be able to reach a settlement before it ever goes to court. Elysium has a wonderful reputation, Vernon," said Irene as she blotted the orange juice from his suit. "People have short memories. You know that expression about today's news lining tomorrow's garbage pails? This will blow over, and Elysium will go on as the miraculous place it's always been."

"Yes, and do *you* know the expression about a picture being worth a thousand words? These pictures will stay in people's minds." Vernon pushed her hand away and stood up. "Either someone who works for me is a traitor or someone who is staying here is responsible for taking these pictures. Either way, I want to know who did this."

He picked up the newspaper again and read the byline on the front-page story. "Anastasia Fernands," he said. "Who the hell is she? I'm going to find out, and when I do, she's going to be one sorry woman."

CHAPTER

29

I T HAD BEEN AN ESPECIALLY miserable morning at the Hollywood Haven Hotel. A tour bus arrived, carrying forty-seven people who were excited about their big trip to the "Land of Movie Stars." Hudson had to check in every one of them. He had no patience for their stupid questions and requests for adjoining rooms.

It was almost noon before he had a chance to look at the newspaper. He pored over every word of the *Times'* account of the murder at Elysium. Hudson felt smugly satisfied that something terrible had happened there. Vernon and Jillian Abernathy had wronged him, and now they were being damaged as they faced the repercussions the murder could have on their business and professional reputations. And if

Jillian had been devastated by the acid attack inflicted on her maid but meant for her, he could only imagine how she was being affected by the murder.

It was some small justice for what the Abernathys had done to his life. But not enough.

"Excuse me."

Hudson looked up from the newspaper. Three middle-aged women were standing on the other side of the registration desk. All were carrying cameras and using their sunglasses as headbands.

"May I help you?" he asked.

"Can you tell us where Marilyn Monroe's star is?" asked the tallest of the three.

"At 6774 Hollywood Boulevard," Hudson answered without missing a beat. The Hollywood Walk of Fame was a tribute to over two thousand artists who had made a contribution to the film, theater, television, radio, and recording industries. Hudson prided himself on knowing the locations of the stars inlaid in the sidewalk for the most famous.

"What about Paul Newman?" asked the chubby one. "I *loved* Paul Newman."

"He's at 7060 Hollywood Boulevard."

"Judy Garland?"

"She's got two," said Hudson, growing impatient. "One for recording at 6764 Hollywood and the other for motion pictures at 1715 Vine Street."

The third woman leaned on the desk and dutifully wrote

down addresses. Hudson could see there was a long list of names. There was no way these hags could expect him to provide the addresses for each star, was there?

The tall woman's next request showed that they expected just that.

"Okay. How about Alfred Hitchcock?" she asked.

"For pity's sake, lady!" Hudson yelled. "Get yourself a map!"

The moment the words were out of his mouth, Hudson knew he'd made a mistake. The women demanded to talk to the manager.

At the end of his shift, Hudson was fired.

CHAPTER

30

AFTER BREAKFAST PIPER WENT BACK to her room to get some sunscreen and her straw hat. The light on the telephone next to her bed was blinking. She called down to the front desk.

"Do I have any messages?" she asked, hoping that Jack had called.

"Yes, Miss Donovan. Miss Abernathy would like you to come over to her cottage."

"Where is it?" asked Piper.

"From the main building, go past the pool and take the path to the right. It's the last one."

"Thanks. Any other messages?"

"No, Miss Donovan. That's all."

THE SCENT OF LAVENDER WAFTED through the air as Piper walked to Jillian's cottage. She passed some of the facilities featured in Elysium's online brochure: the studio where guests could draw, paint, or listen to art-appreciation lectures; the apothecary where guests could create their own custom blends of bath oils and lotions; and the yoga, spinning, and Pilates house, which also included rooms for personal training sessions. The tranquillity and calm were disturbed only by the occasional silent golf cart that passed, carrying passengers dressed in exercise clothes or plush terry-cloth robes—and the men in suits who Piper surmised were police detectives.

At the end of the long path, cactus, agave, sedum, and other moisture-filled succulents covered the ground in front of a stuccoed, southwestern-style cottage. Piper was about to knock when the wood-and-wrought-iron door opened. Jillian stood there, looking very different from the way she had when Piper met her the day before. The skin around her eyes was swollen, her nose was red, and her smooth complexion was blotchy.

"I was watching out the window for you, Piper," she said. "I'm so glad you're here."

Piper walked inside and took in her surroundings. While her suite in the main building was all soothing creams and whites, the living room of the cottage was a more colorful mix of sage green, tan, and turquoise. The furniture was rustic. A Native American–inspired rug covered the floor, and metal art pieces decorated the walls. At the side of the room was a bistro table with two chairs. Piper saw that it was set.

"Have a seat." Jillian gestured. "I went to see my sister yesterday after everything happened. She can always make me feel better, like everything is going to be all right. Nina had her hands full yesterday, though." She managed a wry smile. "Anyway, before I left, I picked up some of the monastery's famous pumpkin bread for you to sample."

As she sat, Piper decided to let Jillian take the lead in the conversation. She wasn't going to bring up Esperanza's murder unless Jillian wanted to talk about it. The bride-to-be was clearly suffering, and Piper didn't want to contribute to any more angst.

Jillian's hand shook as she sliced into the loaf.

Piper reached over and took the knife. "Let me," she said. She cut two pieces and put them on their plates.

"Mmmm. This is absolutely delicious," said Piper after she took the first bite. She chewed carefully, savoring the bread's taste and texture. "I don't know. Maybe we don't even have to change the recipe—with icing on it, I think it could pass as cake. If you wanted to make it less dense, I guess the sisters could adjust the amount of flour, or if you wanted it sweeter, they could add more sugar. But I think it's fabulous just the way it is."

Jillian's face brightened a bit. "It *is* good, isn't it?"

As they ate, Piper asked Jillian questions about the wedding. "Where will the ceremony itself be?"

"There are lots of pretty places on the grounds here," said Jillian, without much enthusiasm in her voice. "But we think the gazebo might be the best spot. That way Ben and I would be on a raised platform and the guests would be able to see us more easily."

Piper smiled. "I was admiring the gazebo when I had breakfast. In fact, I met your fiancé as I was sketching a picture of it."

"Ben's a great guy," said Jillian. "He's been so patient with me and so willing to listen to all my concerns and fears. Sometimes I have to remind myself that I want to be his wife, not his patient. I love him so, and I look forward to our life together—if we can ever get past all this." She shook her head and looked at Piper. "How about you? When you're decorating other people's wedding cakes, you must be thinking about what yours will look like someday."

Piper shrugged. "There *is* someone, but things are a little tense between us right now. I'm starting to realize that I miss him."

"Well, I hope it works out for you," said Jillian.

They had almost finished eating when there was a knock at the front door. Jillian jumped.

"Forgive me," she said. "I'm so on edge. The slightest thing startles me these days."

She got up and looked out the front window. "It's my

stepmother," she said as she walked to the door. "She's been such a doll through all this. I don't know what I'd do without her. She's trying so hard to stand in for my mother. She's even putting together a hope chest for me."

"Darling!" Piper heard the voice before she saw the face. "How are you today, Jillian? Feeling better?"

"Come in, Irene," said Jillian, moving back to make way for Irene to enter. "I want you to meet Piper Donovan."

The attractive older woman came straight at Piper. "Oh, our wedding-cake maker! Wonderful to meet you. Jillian showed me that cake you made for that soap-opera star. Beautiful, just beautiful."

Piper rose to shake hands. She remembered Jillian saying that her stepmother had wanted to use a local baker, yet right now Irene Abernathy didn't look like she was anything but happy to see Piper.

"I'm sorry, dear," said Irene. "I can't shake your hand. My nail polish isn't totally dry yet."

"No problem," said Piper.

"What are you having here?" asked Irene, looking at the table. "A little tea party?"

"Piper was trying the pumpkin bread," said Jillian. "She thinks it might be good enough just the way it is for our wedding cake."

Irene looked surprised. "Really?"

"Of course, it really only matters that Jillian and Ben like it," said Piper. "They're the ones who have to be into it. Plus, we haven't tried any adjusted recipe that the sisters might come up with." She turned to Jillian. "I'd love to go to the Monastery of the Angels, see where they bake, and find out if they have any ideas about how we can make this work."

"Mother Prioress has already okayed making an exception and letting you see the kitchen," said Jillian. "Nobody from the outside world is usually allowed, but because we're hoping to spread the word about their wonderful bakery and candy kitchen, they're praying that it will lead to more people buying their products. The money they make is what keeps the place going, and as you can imagine, times are tough. My sister Nina—I mean, Sister Mary Noelle—will be your guide."

"Would it be possible to go today?" Piper asked eagerly.

Jillian heaved a deep sigh. Then she looked at her stepmother. "Would you be able to take Piper to the convent, Irene?" she asked. "I'm wiped out. I just don't feel up to it."

Irene smiled. "Of course, darling. I've told you over and over. I want to do anything I can to help. Oh, and I took the dress to the bridal shop for alterations. It will be all ready in time for the wedding."

Jillian turned to Piper. "See what I mean?" she asked.

CHAPTER

31

K YLE QUIGLEY TOOK INVENTORY OF the bottles of lotion and jars of cream on the shelves in the treatment room. Counting each container, he made notes on his clipboard. He calculated how much stock he had to order for the month ahead.

He finished too quickly. He had welcomed the usually boring task because it had taken his mind off Esperanza's murder.

Kyle checked the clock. He wasn't looking forward to being interviewed by the police detectives who were methodically questioning Elysium staff and guests. His turn was coming. The last thing he needed was police scrutiny.

As he booted up the computer and began filling in the orders he needed to place, Kyle was sick with guilt and remorse. Esperanza was dead because of what he'd done. She'd told him she had remembered something about the acid attack. Why had he told anyone? Why hadn't he kept his big mouth shut?

Kyle knew he had a problem with gossip. It had gotten him into trouble before. He'd actually lost a couple of friends because they'd felt betrayed when they found out that he'd talked about their private business with other people.

He wondered why he continued to do it when it could be so destructive. He suspected it was because it made him feel important to share news that almost nobody else knew.

Knowledge was power, but this time he'd gone too far. And he was terrified that someday he might get carried away, make a slip, and reveal the dirty secret that lay buried in his own conscience.

CHAPTER

32

I THINK WE'RE GOING TO GET there in time for midday prayer in the chapel," said Irene as she drove Piper down the curving road that led from Elysium toward the city and the Monastery of the Angels. "It's really quite something, Piper. Would you like to hear them pray?"

"Ordinary people can go?" Piper asked with surprise.

"Oh, yes," said Irene. "The public is welcome. But they don't see the nuns. They're hidden behind a screen. At various hours all the nuns assemble in the chapel, but there's at least one of them praying there at all times. They take turns throughout the day and night adoring the Lord exposed on the altar in the form of the Host."

"Wow," Piper mused, "I can't imagine living my life like

that. But it's kind of comforting to know there are people who live their lives just to pray."

"Yes, but I can't imagine it either," said Irene as she turned off the freeway. "I enjoy the outside world too much. I like eating in fine restaurants and attending fun parties and getting massages and buying beautiful clothes. Just think of all the things the nuns give up."

"I don't know," said Piper. "It could be liberating, not having to worry about all the physical stuff, just concentrating on the spiritual."

"Well, it certainly isn't for everybody," said Irene. "I remember when Nina announced she was going to be a nun. Vernon was beside himself."

"How long ago was that?" asked Piper.

"About three years ago," answered Irene. "A few months after her mother died, Nina decided she was going into the convent. Everyone's heart went out to the whole family when Caryn passed away. She was an absolutely beautiful woman, inside and out."

As the car turned off Franklin Avenue, Piper pointed through the windshield. "Look!" she exclaimed. "The Hollywood sign!"

Piper couldn't believe how excited she was. She had seen the iconic sign hundreds of times on television and in movies and magazines, but it was a thrill to see it in person. The worldwide symbol of the entertainment industry had letters forty-five feet high and was planted proudly in rough, steep terrain in the Hollywood Hills. When the car reached the next corner, the sign looked as though it stood right over the Monastery of the Angels.

"That's kind of weird, isn't it?" said Piper.

Irene shrugged. "I never really thought about it before, but I guess it *is* sort of an ironic juxtaposition."

The monastery, complete with a bell tower, sat on almost four acres. The building, with its terra-cotta roof tiles, had once been the estate of a copper magnate, and eventually became the first monastery of cloistered nuns in Southern California. A chapel had been added on the side, and an art deco silver angel stood guard over the parking lot.

Piper and Irene got out of the car and walked across the macadam. At one end of the parking lot was a small shrine. Bouquets of flowers had been placed at the feet of a religious statue. Off the lot there was a cement courtyard with a tall pine tree growing in the middle and bronze plaques depicting the Stations of the Cross affixed to the cinder-block walls. Piper noticed barbed wire spread across the top.

"That isn't there to keep the nuns in, is it?" she asked.

Irene smiled. "I think the idea is to keep the bad guys *out*."

They passed through a covered walkway that led to the Chapel of Perpetual Adoration. As they opened the door and entered, organ music was playing. A few people were scattered throughout the small church. Piper and Irene took seats in one of the many empty pews.

Light filtered in through the modern stained-glass windows. The altar was simple, but an exquisite golden monstrance sat atop it. On the far side of the altar, a divider was decorated with candles, and behind that was a tall screen. Piper could hear women's voices coming from the other side of the screen.

While she said a prayer for Esperanza and for her own parents, her brother, and even her sister-in-law, the nuns sang. Fifteen minutes of singing was followed by reading and quiet contemplation, punctuated by an occasional anonymous cough. After a final prayer, the lights behind the screen went off, and Piper could hear the nuns shuffling away to the refectory and their main meal of the day.

Irene signaled for Piper to follow her. "Sister Mary Noelle should be in the gift shop now," she whispered.

They exited the chapel and walked along the side of a quiet garden. When they reached the entrance to the gift shop, Irene rang the bell beside the wrought-iron door. A tall woman, wearing a simple white dress, a belt with rosary beads attached, and a short black veil, appeared and welcomed them inside. The woman was very pretty, her face unlined and makeup-free. Piper could instantly see the resemblance to Jillian.

Irene made the introductions.

"It's good to meet you, Piper," said Sister Mary Noelle. "I'm so glad Jillian has you to help make her wedding day special. She has been through so much, and I pray that the day my sister and Ben are married goes as well as she so richly deserves."

"I hope so, too, Sister," said Piper. "I've got to tell you that you're making my life so much easier! With you baking the cake, all I have to do is decorate it."

The nun smiled. "We are going to need you, Piper, to show us how to assemble it. When the layers are as large as I think you'll want them to be, I would think you can't just stack them one on top of the other."

Piper nodded. "No, we'll need supports, but it won't be hard to do."

"All right, then," said Sister Mary Noelle as she gestured to a door at the rear of the room. "Let me show you our kitchen."

Piper and Irene started walking.

"Oh, Irene," said the sister, "I'm sorry, but Mother gave permission only for Piper to enter."

"Surely she wouldn't mind if I joined you," said Irene.

The nun looked uncomfortable. "I'm sorry, but Mother isn't available right now, and I'd never presume to amend the specific permission she gave me."

Irene's face registered disappointment, but she quickly composed herself. "No problem," she said. "I'll wait out in the garden for you, Piper."

No one else was in the kitchen.

"All the sisters are having their dinner, and after that

they will observe an hour of silence for midday rest and contemplation," explained Sister Mary Noelle.

Piper looked around. Everything looked familiar. The kitchen was outfitted in much the same way as her mother's bakery. A large refrigerator and stove, an industrial-size electric mixer, sacks of flour and sugar waiting to be opened, and shining stainless-steel bowls stacked neatly on long worktables. Just like The Icing on the Cupcake.

"I think the only things we're missing are the large round baking pans," said Piper after she had checked out the cabinets and drawers. "And I'll also get the wooden dowels to support and fasten the graduated cake layers. I've brought my piping tips and other paraphernalia with me from New Jersey. Other than that, all we need to decide is whether you sisters will amend your recipe or if we'll go with the original pumpkin bread. I had some this morning, and it definitely tastes good enough to be cake."

Sister Mary Noelle opened the refrigerator door, took out a shopping bag, and handed it to Piper. "The sisters have tried a few variations," she said. "There are samples inside. Would you take them to Jillian and Ben? All three of you can taste and decide."

Just as they were about to leave, an older nun appeared at the kitchen door. Sister Mary Noelle introduced Piper to the prioress.

Mother Mary Dominic nodded and smiled pleasantly. "Nice to meet you, Piper. I hope that we'll be able to help you. The Abernathys have been very generous to us, and we are happy if we can help in some small way." She turned to Sister Mary Noelle. "Is that Mrs. Abernathy I saw waiting outside?" she asked.

"Yes, Mother, that's my father's wife."

"Well, you certainly know, Sister, that she would be welcome in our kitchen, too."

Sister Mary Noelle's face reddened slightly. "We're finished here anyway, Mother," she said.

CHAPTER

33

N ICE WORK, ANASTASIA. YOUR STORY was great and the pictures and video were terrific. We're blowing everybody away on this thing."

Still in her terry-cloth robe, Anastasia lounged on her bed, propped up with a pile of down pillows. There was a copy of the *L.A. Times* on her lap. She had already read her story on the murder of Esperanza Flores three times. She held the phone to her ear and smiled with satisfaction at the praise coming from her editor.

"Glad you're pleased, Tim," she said. "I have to tell you that it's a thrill to see my byline on the front page. That's a first for me."

"Yeah, well, keep up the good work and it won't be the last," said the editor. "And don't forget our Web site. We'll post any good video you get. Who knows where else it will end up! *Good Morning America* used some of it today."

When she ended the call, Anastasia congratulated herself on having the foresight to register at Elysium using a different last name, with a credit card she'd kept active after her divorce from Jeff Wilcox. If the Abernathys knew that it was she who was responsible for the press coverage, they undoubtedly would have asked her to leave. She had to remain on the inside to cover the aftermath of the murder as well as to finish her research on the story that had brought her here in the first place.

Anastasia picked up the spa directory from the table and perused the contents. She ached to take a yoga class or get a massage to relieve the tension in her neck and shoulders. But she decided it would be in the best interest of her story to call the skin-treatment room for an appointment.

"Is Kyle Quigley available to do my facial?" she asked. "I hear he's the best."

CHAPTER

34

Monday, Wednesday, and Friday afternoons at three, Wendy Ellis had a standing appointment. The sessions with Dr. Ben Dixon were the focal points of her week. Those were virtually the only times she ventured out of her cottage. If she could have talked Dr. Ben into coming to her instead of going to see him in his office, she would have. But he insisted that she come to him.

Wendy suspected that it wasn't really essential that the therapy be conducted at his place in the main building. Dr. Ben just wanted her to leave the safety of her cottage. He was always encouraging her to get out more and telling her that she would feel better if she interacted with the world. It wasn't healthy to be alone all the time.

"But I'm not alone," Wendy protested as she sat in his office Friday afternoon. "My father comes to see me every day. Dr. Abernathy comes to check on me during the week, the kitchen people bring me my food, and I see people once in a while when I walk over here to see you."

"Do you talk to any of them?"

Wendy looked down at her lap. "Not really," she said. "I only talk to my dad, you, and Dr. Abernathy."

"You're living a very isolated existence, Wendy," said Dr. Ben. "That was fine for a while. You were wounded."

"I still am," said Wendy, reaching up to feel the cotton mask she wore to cover the place where her nose had been. "I have to face the fact that I always will be. I don't want anyone to look at me." Her brown eyes filled with tears.

"What exactly are you afraid of?" he asked.

Wendy thought for a moment, her eyes focused on the painting on the wall. "I'm afraid people will be disgusted, that they'll think I'm a monster," she whispered. "*I* think I'm a monster."

"Let me ask you something else, Wendy. Say you were walking down the street and you saw someone approaching who looked like you—how would *you* react?"

"With the mask or without?" she asked.

"Both," said Dr. Ben.

Wendy shrugged. "I guess if I saw somebody walking toward me with a mask on, if they weren't dressed like a low-life or I didn't get the feeling that they were going to attack me or something, I'd think that they were wearing the mask because of the smog or because they were afraid of germs or something like that."

"And if you saw somebody without the mask?" asked Dr. Ben.

"I'd be grossed out."

"Would you think the person was a monster?"

"No, I guess not," said Wendy. "I guess I'd just feel sorry for the person and be glad it wasn't me."

"So you'd feel compassion for that person, right?"

Wendy nodded.

Dr. Ben leaned forward in his chair. "Wendy, do you think you can try? Can you give your fellow human beings the benefit of the doubt and trust that they will react as you would?"

For a full minute, Wendy said nothing. Dr. Ben waited for her answer. Finally she spoke.

"Maybe I can try to go out," she said slowly. "With my mask on, of course."

Dr. Ben smiled. "Good," he said. "That's a start. When you come next time, you can tell me about what you did and the people you talked with and what you thought their reactions were. Try to go out and talk to someone new at least once today, tomorrow, and Sunday. You're ready, Wendy."

CHAPTER

35

W HEN PIPER RETURNED TO ELYSIUM from the convent, she went to her suite and checked the spa directory to see if there was some sort of class she could take in the late afternoon. There was a yoga class at four o'clock. She washed her face, changed quickly, and headed out again.

Forgoing the elevator, she hurried down the staircase to the ground floor. As she opened the door, she almost bumped into the person coming out of the office across the hallway.

"Oh, sorry," said Piper. "I shouldn't have been in such a rush."

"No problem," murmured the young woman, keeping her head lowered.

Both of them walked down the hallway alongside each other. When they got to the door, Piper leaned forward, opened it, and held it.

"After you," she said, smiling and trying to make eye contact.

"Thank you." The girl didn't look at Piper as she passed through.

They continued walking in the same direction.

"I'm going to try one of the yoga classes," said Piper. "Have you been?"

"No." The girl hesitated. "I'm going back to my cottage."

"Oh, I've seen a couple of the cottages. They're really amazing. Do you love yours?"

"It's fine, I guess."

"How long are you staying?" asked Piper.

"I don't really know."

Piper wondered what was under the girl's mask. Had she had some sort of treatment that needed to be covered as it healed? Was she allergic to something? Though curious, Piper wasn't going to ask.

As if anticipating the question and bracing herself for it, the girl straightened up and looked directly into Piper's eyes. "I had some surgery that went really wrong," she blurted.

"That's terrible," said Piper. "I'm so sorry."

"Thanks." The girl sighed with relief. "Now that that's over with, I don't have to talk to anyone else till tomorrow."

Piper looked at her, puzzled.

The girl's eyes crinkled at the edges. Piper could tell she was smiling beneath the mask.

"My therapist says I have to talk to someone every day. You just filled my assignment for Friday."

"Oh, well, I'm glad I could help," said Piper. "You know, I'm here by myself. If you want, I'd love to have some company. Do you want to have dinner together?"

The girl answered swiftly. "Oh, no, I couldn't go to the dining room with all those . . . people."

"Well, how about the patio? I had breakfast there this morning, and I was the only one out there."

"That's really nice of you to ask." The girl hesitated again. "What's your name?"

"Piper."

"I'm Wendy. Anyway, I don't think dinner is a good idea for me."

"Okay, but if you change your mind, or if you want to have breakfast or lunch or whatever, I'm in room 307. Just call me."

CHAPTER

36

A PRETTY BRUNETTE SAT ACROSS the dinner table from Jack. Her blue eyes were focused on him alone. She was clearly intelligent and a good conversationalist, up on what was happening in the world. She laughed at his humor. There was nothing wrong with the way she held her fork or chewed her food.

Why couldn't he just like this girl? Why did he keep thinking about Piper?

Jack downed a second glass of wine. Then another. By the time the waiter came to take their dessert orders, the brunette seemed more appealing.

"After we're through here, want to go downtown for a nightcap?" he asked.

"Downtown where?" asked the young woman.

"There's a comedy club in the Village that's fun or . . ." Jack hesitated.

"Or what?"

"We could go to my apartment."

The brunette leaned back in her chair and smiled. "You know what, Jack? I think I'll pass."

"Really?"

"Yeah, really. I'm a big believer in chemistry, something you feel, right from the start. No offense, Jack, but I'm not feeling it tonight. I've gotten the sense that you weren't even really here. Your mind was somewhere else."

CHAPTER

37

L IGHTS WERE OUT AT NINE-FIFTEEN.
While she truly loved being with her sisters in community all day long, Sister Mary Noelle also treasured her time alone at night. Her monastic cell was spartan, with a single bed, a table, and a desk. Only the necessities for rest and prayer, meditation, study, and individual work. A crucifix hung over the bed. The other walls were bare.

Sister Mary Noelle was relieved that the day was over. Whenever she had to deal with seeing her father's wife, it sapped her of energy and caused inner turmoil. She struggled with her complicated feelings about Irene.

The nun removed her veil and took off her habit, hanging it up carefully. She slipped on a simple white nightgown. Taking her rosary from the desk and sinking to her

knees beside the small bed, she bowed her head and began
to pray.

> *Heavenly Father, please help me. I strive, but I
> always come up short. Help me make my peace with
> my father and Irene. You know how much I love my
> father, Lord. Please, help me to forgive him. I know
> it was an accident. My father loved my mother; he
> would never have intentionally hurt her. I want to
> let go of the anger I know I still harbor toward him.
> Dear God, please help me to do that.*

The floor was hard beneath her knees. Sister Mary
Noelle didn't mind the discomfort; she could offer it up for
the poor souls in purgatory. She continued her prayer.

> *Help me to accept Irene, dear Jesus. I know she loves
> my father and does her best to make him happy.
> Please, help me to stop judging her. Release me from
> the unkind thoughts I have about her. I am ashamed
> of myself that I continue to dwell on things that
> happened years ago.*

The nun let her rosary beads dangle from her fingers.
Her mouth moved intermittently as she recited the Hail
Marys and Our Fathers. When she finished her prayers, she
crossed herself and kissed the crucifix at the end of the beads.
Then she remembered one last prayer.

Help Jillian see, Lord. Help her understand how important it is that she and Ben be married in a church by a priest. A gazebo at Elysium isn't the place to receive the holy sacrament of matrimony.

Sister Mary Noelle got up from her knees and pulled back the blanket on top of the bed. Though bone tired, she hesitated before getting in. *Why do I feel compelled to look at it again?*

She went to the desk and slid open the bottom drawer. Beneath the paperwork she was required to do for the gift shop, she found the long white envelope. She pulled out and reread the letter she just couldn't bring herself to rip up or throw away.

CHAPTER

38

*J*ILLIAN IS JUST A WEEK *away from being a bride. And a beautiful one she'll be unless she's stopped. If that gorgeous face is marred, if that blond mane is scorched, all bets are off. The wedding probably won't take place at all.*

The acid didn't find its mark, but fire can be equally destructive and horribly maiming. Burns can produce the most grotesque scars. Sometimes, if the burns are too severe, the victim dies.

Maybe death should be the aim after all. If Jillian is merely disfigured . . . that might not be enough.

The turpentine is ready and waiting. All that's needed now is the opportunity.

CHAPTER

39

PIPER WOKE UP EARLY, HER internal clock still on East Coast time. She showered, dressed, and went down to breakfast. Afterward she stopped in the communications room, where computers were set up for the spa's guests.

Her conversation with Irene Abernathy and their trip the day before to the Monastery of the Angels had piqued Piper's interest again in the death of Caryn Collins Abernathy. She'd been meaning to find out more about it since she first saw it mentioned in the online article about Jillian. But with the rush to get ready for her trip and the busy first days at Elysium, she'd forgotten.

With the stroke of a few keys and a click of the mouse, Piper was engrossed in a flurry of stories that had run in newspapers, trade publications, and even a medical journal.

She read that Caryn, forty-five, had died of complications following plastic surgery performed by her husband, Vernon Abernathy, M.D. An autopsy had been performed, indicating that the otherwise very healthy female had died of cardiac arrest suffered while she was in the recovery room.

An article that ran in *Variety* focused on Caryn, listing her professional accomplishments, mostly commercials and smaller roles in episodic television. The picture that ran with the article showed a beautiful blonde with high cheekbones and expressive eyes. Piper observed that Jillian's and Sister Mary Noelle's resemblance to their mother was unmistakable.

The point of the medical journal's article was about the ethics of physicians treating family members. The American Medical Association maintained that "physicians generally should not treat themselves or members of their immediate family." Yet, according to the article, a survey showed that a significant number of doctors did just that, prescribing medication, diagnosing illness, and doing physical examinations. A small percentage even admitted to performing surgery on someone in their family. The Abernathy case was noted as a cautionary tale. Vernon Abernathy himself had been interviewed for the article.

"Even as I agreed to do Caryn's surgery, I knew I shouldn't. I was too close. But Caryn was determined to have her face lifted. She said she trusted only me, that I was the best. I shouldn't have given in, but I suppose I liked believing that I would do the best job. I wanted to be her hero.

"Now I wonder. If somebody else had done the surgery, would Caryn still be alive? Would she have suffered the heart attack anyway? I'll never know, but I can't help feeling responsible. It eats away at me."

Hearing the door to the communications room open, Piper turned. She recognized Anastasia, the woman she'd met at the pool the first afternoon, the woman she suspected might be a reporter. Piper clicked the mouse to make the story on the computer screen disappear.

"Hey, Piper. How's it going?" asked Anastasia as she took a seat in front of one of the other computers.

"Fine, thanks," said Piper, impressed that the woman remembered her name. "You know, I realized I didn't get your last name when we met the other day."

"I didn't give it." She reached out to shake Piper's hand. "But it's Wilcox. Anastasia Wilcox." Sliding over to her computer, she said, "I heard there was a piece on the Esperanza Flores murder on *Good Morning America* yesterday. I missed it, and I want to see it."

"My father told me about it, but I didn't catch it either," said Piper. "I'd like to see it, too."

The ABC News Web site came up on Anastasia's screen. They waited while the fifteen-second commercial ran before the story began. Piper glanced at Anastasia and noticed the slight smile on her face as the somewhat shaky video that led the piece started to run.

"It looks like somebody shot that with a cell phone, doesn't it?" asked Piper.

Anastasia nodded, still concentrating on the story.

"Man, the people who own this place must hate this," said Piper.

"You think so?" Anastasia asked absentmindedly.

"Sure," said Piper. "I mean, think about it. Somebody who works here or is staying here took pictures that don't exactly cast Elysium in the best light and then went ahead and sold them. It must be humiliating."

"I don't know," said Anastasia as the piece ended. "It's news. If something happened, it happened. There's nothing wrong with reporting it. In fact, the public deserves to know."

"Sure," said Piper. "But they have a no-cameras policy thing here. At the very least, whoever took the pictures violated that."

Anastasia held out her hands and shrugged. "Yeah, well, what can you do?"

The expression of satisfaction on her face gave her away. In that instant, Piper decided to go ahead and say it.

"I have a feeling you're the one who took that video, Anastasia."

"You do, huh?"

Piper nodded. "Are you a reporter?" she asked.

Anastasia sat back in her chair. "Why would you ask me that?"

"Because I overheard you on your cell phone at the pool. You were talking about amazing pictures, and then I saw you typing with that wire in your ear. So when I heard that a video showed up on *GMA,* I thought you might have taken it."

Anastasia was silent as she considered Piper's words. Finally she put her finger to her lips and slid closer to Piper. She answered, her voice low. "If I tell you, will you promise to keep it to yourself?"

Automatically, Piper nodded.

"Yes, I am a reporter. My real name is Fernands. Anastasia Fernands. I'm here working on an investigative piece. I'm not sure if it's directly related to Esperanza's murder or not. But when I heard about what had happened at Cottage 7, I hurried over and instinctively wanted to cover the story."

Piper was a little surprised that Anastasia had been so forthcoming. "And you're telling me this because . . . ?"

"I'm telling you for two reasons," said Anastasia. "One, you practically had it figured out already, so there was no point in denying it. And two, I might need a little help."

CHAPTER

40

FORTUNATELY, THERE HADN'T BEEN ANOTHER story written by Anastasia Fernands in the *Times*. The day-two follow-up story had run on page 5, written by staff journalists.

Vernon laid down the newspaper and picked up the report he'd been expecting, then scowled as he studied its contents. The list of spa guests had been carefully checked. There was no Anastasia Fernands on it. There was, however, an Anastasia Wilcox.

He was about to make a phone call when he heard a knock at the door.

"Come in," he called. As the door opened, his facial expression changed. "Jillian," he said with pleasure. "Come in, my darling."

Jillian came over to the desk and kissed her father on the cheek. "Hi, Dad. How's it going?"

"Better, now that you're here," he said. "Are *you* feeling better today, honey?"

Jillian forced a weak smile. "Life has to go on, doesn't it?" she asked.

"Absolutely, honey," answered Vernon, gesturing for his daughter to sit. "I want you to try not to think about everything that's happened. Just concentrate on your wedding. You'll be doing us all a favor. We need something positive around here."

"Have you heard anything from the police?" asked Jillian.

"Apparently the coroner found skin under Esperanza's fingernails, skin they think she scratched as she fought off her killer. But that will help only if the killer's DNA is already in the database," said Vernon. "The detectives are returning today to interview the rest of the staff and guests. I've already had more than one of our VIP guests come in to complain about being questioned. People feel that their privacy is being violated, since many of them don't even want anyone to know they're at Elysium."

"Oh, Dad. This is all so hard on you."

"Don't worry about me," said Vernon. "I'm fine. I'm on a mission, though, and maybe that's a good thing. It's keeping my mind off Esperanza. I had grown so fond of her."

"I know you had, Daddy. I think Irene's idea about a memorial service for Esperanza is a good one. It will make all of us feel a little better."

Vernon loved it when Jillian slipped into her childhood name for him. He missed the days when Jillian and Nina were young and he and Caryn had been so happy together. Things were much simpler then. Irene tried hard, but she was no Caryn. Every time he looked at Jillian, he was reminded of how much he still loved her mother.

Jillian perceived wistfulness in her father's expression. "What are you thinking about, Dad?" she asked.

Vernon shook his head slightly. "Oh, nothing," he lied. Then he said, "I was thinking about finding the person who ignored our rules and took those pictures that ended up all over the place."

"Any luck with that?"

"So far, no," said Vernon. "But there may be one lead—a guest named Anastasia Wilcox. I'm going to make sure that we have her watched."

CHAPTER

41

HER EYES SHONE OVER THE rim of her mask, and it was the first time in months that George Ellis had detected any happiness in his daughter's voice. He arrived at the cottage on Saturday morning to find Wendy waiting for him, eager to tell him her news.

"I met someone yesterday, a guest here. And she actually talked to me, Dad! She didn't look disgusted—in fact, she didn't even seem to care at all that I look the way I do. And she asked me if I wanted to have dinner with her!"

"Did you?" George asked hopefully.

"No," said Wendy. "But she said that if I ever wanted to have somebody to eat with, I should call. I can't believe it."

"What can't you believe?" asked her father.

"That a stranger would think she'd be able to sit across the table from me and not feel like throwing up."

George put his arms around his daughter, his heart twisting at the thought of her gratitude, wonder, and excitement over a simple human gesture that most people would hardly notice.

"Oh, Wendy, Wendy, my precious Wendy," he said softly as he stroked her curly red hair. "I'm glad you met someone new and that she was nice to you. But, sweetheart, I hope you believe that you are totally worthy of being liked."

"I don't feel that way, Dad. I don't know if I ever will."

CHAPTER

42

PIPER AND ANASTASIA LEFT THE communications room and walked outside to the meditation garden. They had it to themselves. Still, Anastasia spoke in a very low voice as she explained to Piper the story she was researching.

"I have a friend who made an appointment for a facial with Kyle Quigley, the paramedical aesthetician here at Elysium. While he was working on her face, Quigley told her about this special treatment he'd developed, which he was confident would improve the texture of her skin and make her look fresher and younger. He said it would tone her skin, tighten it, and erase some fine lines she had."

"Where do I sign up?" asked Piper.

"As if you need something like that yet," said Anastasia, shaking her head. "Look at your skin. It doesn't have a freckle, a blemish, or a wrinkle on it. How old are you, anyway?"

"Twenty-seven," said Piper. "And I'm a freak about not going out in the sun."

"Smart girl," said Anastasia. "Anyway, Quigley said the treatment involved being put to sleep, because it was necessary that all her muscles be relaxed and that she not move while he applied this miracle cream. He told her that he thought three treatments would do wonders for her. When she told him she was staying at the spa for only one more day, Quigley said she could come to see him as a day client. She signed up."

Piper squinted as she watched and listened to Anastasia. The morning sun was bright, and she imagined the rays burning the top layer of her skin. She wished she had her sunscreen, hat, and sunglasses.

"I'm sorry, but can we move?" she asked. "I can't even concentrate in this sun. Let's go to the bench under that tree."

When they were settled in the shade, Anastasia continued, fluffing her short dark hair with her fingers. "So my friend went for the first treatment. Quigley gave her some sort of shot to make her sleep, and when she woke up, all she knew was that her skin felt wonderful. There was some redness, but Quigley assured her that that would subside in an hour or two—which it did."

"You know," said Piper, "I've looked at the spa's list of treatments pretty closely. I didn't see a mention of any sort of sleep treatment."

"No," said Anastasia. "There isn't. And here's why. My

friend had another sleep treatment, and when she woke up, she sensed that something was wrong. The button above the zipper on her slacks was missing, and a few hours later she noticed an unexplained bruise on her inner thigh. She was creeped out."

"Uh-oh," said Piper, immediately thinking back to her college days. "I remember my college roommate, Sarah, going home over Christmas break her junior year. She had to have her wisdom teeth removed. It turns out that the dentist fondled her while she was under anesthesia."

Anastasia nodded.

"In just a few weeks, she went from being fun and outgoing to being moody and remote," Piper said. "The rest of college was tough. I remember she had trouble sleeping, her grades dropped, and she lost all interest in going out with guys.

"The last time I talked to her, she was still in therapy. That sicko did more than cop a feel. He wrecked a young woman's life."

"It was criminal," said Anastasia.

"So you think Kyle Quigley is sedating clients and molesting them while they're out of it?"

"Something like that," answered Anastasia. "That's what I'm trying to find out anyway. But when I went to see him yesterday, I struck out, Piper. He said I wasn't a candidate for this sleep treatment. When I asked him why, he gave me some line about my skin being too sun-damaged." She looked pointedly at Piper, her eyes sweeping over Piper's white arms. "That's certainly something he could never say to *you*, Piper."

CHAPTER

43

G EORGE AND WENDY PLAYED THEIR fourth game of Scrab-ble. They had both become quite proficient in making the most of every double-letter and triple-word score. They played almost every day. It passed the time.

"V-I-T-R-I-O-L. 'Vitriol,'" said Wendy, putting down all her tiles. "And it lands on the double-word score."

"Plus the extra fifty points for using all your letters," said her father.

"And don't forget the two points for 'la,'" said Wendy, pointing to the word formed by the *l* of "vitriol" sitting above the *a* in "ark."

"Good for you, honey," he said. "I'm impressed."

"I have a lot of time on my hands, Dad. Sometimes I just

flip through the Scrabble dictionary and learn new words and their meanings. I call it 'continuing ed.'"

George looked at his daughter with concern. "You're so close to getting your degree, Wendy," he said gently, broaching what he knew to be a touchy subject. "Have you been thinking any more about going back to school and finishing up?"

"As a matter of fact, I have," said Wendy as she wrote down her score on the pad.

George brightened. "Really? That's terrific, Wendy!"

"Yeah, I was looking, and I think I'll be able to complete the credits I need online," she said happily. "I don't even have to travel to campus."

WHEN GEORGE LEFT THE COTTAGE, he was seething. The fact that his daughter now based what she did in life on the ability to avoid other human beings was gut-wrenching. No parent should have to watch his child struggling with the physical and emotional pain that Wendy did.

He could choose to be brokenhearted, or he could choose to be angry. George chose anger. He could picture the man who had devastated Wendy's life going on his merry way. Vernon Abernathy's beautiful daughter was getting married next week with her whole life ahead of her, while George's daughter was afraid to leave her safe little cottage. That was wrong.

Abernathy had even sent that ridiculous e-mail invitation to the wedding. Did Vernon think he was a fool? George saw the invitation for what it was—Vernon's pathetic attempt to ingratiate himself. They weren't friends. They never would be. And a wedding invitation wasn't going to be the thing to dissuade George from legal remedies against Vernon.

George wondered again how Vernon Abernathy would feel if his daughter Jillian's face was destroyed.

CHAPTER

44

FOR THE FIRST SATURDAY MORNING in forever, the alarm hadn't been set. Hudson reveled in the luxury of staying in bed until noon. He lay there all morning, drowsing on and off. In the periods while he was awake, he thought about how happy he was not to be employed any longer at the Hollywood Haven Hotel. He'd hated that place and the lowly position he'd been forced to hold there.

Hudson realized that unemployment benefits would last only so long. Eventually he'd have to find another job. He knew where he wanted to work.

The acid attack, Esperanza Flores's murder, and the upcoming wedding must be stretching Jillian thin and, he hoped, were all too much for her to handle. Though it might be premature to think that Jillian wouldn't want to be Elysium's director anymore, at least Vernon might see that his daughter needed some help. Once Hudson was back on the inside, he might be able to cultivate more responsibility and eventually get his directorship back.

It was worth a shot.

He still had Vernon's private number. Hudson decided he was going to call him today and see if Vernon would meet with him. If he had to, he would beg.

When he finally dragged himself out of bed, Hudson went to the bathroom. He washed his hands and opened the linen closet to grab a faded towel. As he looked over the contents of the closet, he noted that almost all of the supplies he'd taken with him when he left Elysium were gone now. He had used up every bar of hand-milled soap, every bottle of lotion, and every jar of soothing cream. All that was left was the box of peach-colored latex gloves.

CHAPTER

45

A CAR AND DRIVER WERE AT Piper's disposal. She had the driver take her to a bakery-supply store, where she purchased round baking pans in graduated sizes and wooden dowels to support the layers. From there they went to the supermarket, and Piper bought confectioners' sugar, butter, vanilla extract, and cream cheese. Her plan was to make her mother's cream-cheese icing and serve it atop the samples of pumpkin cake that Sister Mary Noelle had given her. That way Jillian and Ben would have a real sense of how the cake they chose for their wedding day would taste.

As they drove back to Elysium, Piper considered the story Anastasia had told her and the request she'd made. Piper recoiled at the thought of getting anywhere near Kyle Quigley if what Anastasia suspected about him was true. It was utterly repulsive to think that he was sedating women and then taking advantage of them in some depraved way.

As her anger rose, Piper asked herself if she really wanted to be the one to find out what Kyle was up to. If he was guilty, who knew what Kyle was capable of—especially if he thought someone was onto his shenanigans?

But as she recalled the hell her roommate Sarah had been through when she was a victim of this sort of abuse, Piper felt that helping Anastasia was the right thing to do. If Kyle was doing what Anastasia thought he was, he had to be stopped. Piper couldn't just shrug as if it weren't her problem. If this was really going on, it was everybody's problem.

As Piper looked out the car window, she saw Hollywood High School and, on the next corner, an In-N-Out Burger.

"Excuse me, will you please pull in here?" she asked the driver.

Knowing that her vanilla shake would be pure ice cream, she ordered her burger "protein style," wrapped in lettuce instead of a bun. As she bit into the burger, she thought of Jack and the fun they'd had in their quest to find the best hamburgers in Manhattan. They loved the ones served at Five Napkin Burger. Jack had told her that his favorites in Los Angeles were the ones at Umami Burger and In-N-Out.

Piper had a sudden impulse to call him. But she didn't.

She could just imagine what Jack would say if she told him about getting involved with Anastasia and her investigation. He would remind her that she wasn't in law enforcement or a private detective. She was an actress and a part-time wedding-cake maker. He'd remind her that auditioning for *Law & Order: Special Victims Unit* didn't make her a real-life Olivia Benson.

Maybe Anastasia was right. Piper could just look at this as a role she was playing. What would it hurt simply to see Kyle and ask about the sleep treatment or find out if he suggested it himself? She wasn't making a commitment to be sedated.

Esperanza Flores was murdered. Kyle Quigley could be a sexual predator. Are the two things related?

As the car headed north toward the spa, Piper sipped her milk shake and thought about the last forty-eight hours. Elysium really wasn't turning out to be the paradise that most people thought it was.

CHAPTER

46

I RENE HAD INSISTED THEY HAVE lunch together. Vernon knew she only had his best interests at heart, that she wanted to make sure he stayed healthy. Yet sometimes he felt smothered—and guilty. Though Irene wanted nothing more than to spend time alone together, Vernon needed his space. Never more so than when he was under stress.

He ate his turkey sandwich hurriedly. In between bites he responded to Irene's attempts at conversation with short answers and nods.

"Coffee, dear?" she asked when they'd finished eating.

Vernon lifted the napkin from his lap and laid it on the table. "I'm afraid I don't have time, Irene," he said. "I have to get back to the office."

He gave his wife a perfunctory kiss on the cheek, and then he was gone.

THE SECURITY REPORT WAS WAITING for him on his desk. As Vernon read it, he could see that Anastasia had done almost nothing that seemed suspicious. On Friday she'd spent some time in her room before going for a facial and a long walk on the grounds. She had eaten dinner by herself, ordering a bottle of Nero d'Avola with her grilled salmon, wild rice, and broccoli rabe. She drank two glasses and asked the waiter to cork the bottle, which she took with her when she left the dining room and returned to her quarters.

This morning Anastasia had had two poached eggs, dry toast, and black coffee for breakfast. Afterward she'd gone to the communications room, where she'd spoken with another guest, Piper Donovan. Together they'd watched something on the computer screen. When the women left the room, security checked the computer and found that it had been used to link to the ABC News Web site and the story about the murder at Elysium.

Anastasia and Piper Donovan had spent time talking in the meditation garden before both women went their separate ways. Now Anastasia was at the pool.

All of it seemed benign, except the part about the news piece, which Vernon all too angrily remembered contained the video that no one had any right to record. Had the women been watching the piece with mere curiosity about what had happened at the spa? That would be natural and understandable. Or was there more to it? Was Anastasia gloating as she watched the video that she herself had taken?

Vernon recognized Piper Donovan as the name of the wedding-cake maker Jillian had talked about with such enthusiasm. Vernon had been happy when Jillian had told him that Piper had agreed to come all the way from the East Coast to make the wedding cake his daughter wanted.

But what was this girl doing talking in the meditation garden with the woman who might have betrayed him and could be ruining everything he'd worked on for years?

CHAPTER

47

THERE WERE TWO MESSAGES WAITING for Piper when she got back to Elysium. The first was from Jillian Abernathy saying that she and her fiancé were available to sample the wedding cakes at four o'clock in Jillian's cottage. The second message was from Wendy Ellis.

"Hi, Piper. It's me, Wendy. The one you met yesterday afternoon? I was wondering if you really would like to have dinner with me. I don't know if you still want to, but let me know, okay?"

Piper could hear the hesitancy in the voice. She had a feeling that it took a great deal of effort for Wendy to make that call. Immediately, Piper dialed the extension Wendy had left and agreed to meet her on the patio at six o'clock.

THOUGH IT WAS WELL AFTER lunch and several hours before dinnertime, the kitchen was still an active place. Carrots and celery were being chopped, other vegetables were being roasted, and chicken parts were being skinned and cleaned. Piper scanned the room, looking for a person who appeared to be in charge.

The tall hat tipped her off. Approaching the chef, Piper introduced herself.

"Ah, *oui,*" said the chef. "Miss Jillian said that I should expect you and provide you with whatever you need."

"A mixing bowl, measuring spoons and cups, an electric mixer, and a space to work would be amazing," said Piper. "I've got everything else I need."

"Come, follow me," said the chef.

He led her to a workstation in the corner of the room. Piper deposited her bags on the stainless-steel counter and emptied the contents. Next she stopped to wash her hands at a nearby sink. She unwrapped the cream cheese and butter, put them into the mixing bowl, and proceeded to beat them together until smooth. Then she measured out the vanilla extract and combined it with the creamy mixture. Finally she stirred in the confectioners' sugar gradually. When she was satisfied it was the right consistency, Piper swiped her pinkie through the frosting and sampled it.

"Mmm," she said aloud. *It tastes just like my mother's icing.*

Next she carefully unwrapped the aluminum foil that protected the small round layers of pumpkin cake she'd been given at the convent. She considered merely covering the cakes with simple coats of frosting but thought better of it. She took out her #104 piping tip, a flower nail, and one of the plastic piping bags she'd brought with her. Snipping off the tip of the plastic cone, she attached the piping tip and carefully filled the cone with the cream-cheese icing.

For the next forty-five minutes, she fashioned roses, sweet peas, and bows, covering the tops of the three small cakes. When she was finished, she admired her handiwork.

"Oh, là là."

Piper turned around to see the chef standing behind her, looking over her shoulder and smiling.

"Thanks," she said. "Now, would you happen to have a tray I can put these on to take down to Jillian's cottage?"

"Mais oui," said the chef. "And if there is any left later, I would love to sample some. You are *très* talented."

PIPER WAS SOMEWHAT SURPRISED TO see Irene Abernathy standing at the cottage door.

"Come in, come in," said Irene. "We've been looking forward to this."

Piper carried the tray inside. Jillian, Ben, and a white-haired gentleman she'd never met were seated in the living area. Piper was promptly introduced to Jillian's father, the owner of Elysium.

"Glad to finally meet you, Piper," said Vernon. "I've

heard so much about you. Thank you for coming all this way to make my daughter's wedding cake."

"Thank you for having me," said Piper. "And I've really been enjoying my stay at Elysium."

"You haven't come at the most peaceful time, have you, Piper?" asked Vernon. "I deeply regret that."

"Now, dear," said Irene, waving her hand. "Let's not get into all that dreary business. Right now we have something happy to do. Let's enjoy it."

"You're right, of course, Irene," said Vernon. "Let's see what you've brought for us to try, Piper."

Piper put the tray down on the coffee table while Jillian went to get plates, forks, and napkins.

"Do you want to cut the cakes, Jillian?" asked Piper.

"No, you do it," answered Jillian, smiling weakly. "They're so pretty I hate hacking into them, and besides, I'm saving my cake-cutting skills for our wedding day." She looked up at her fiancé. Ben reached over, put his arm around her, and kissed her on the cheek.

As everyone watched, Piper took the serving knife and sliced into the first cake, dividing the circle into quarters. Her hand trembled slightly, and she realized she was a little nervous.

"Is everything all right, Piper?" asked Vernon. He was smiling, but Piper sensed that he was scrutinizing her every move.

"A trifle nervous, I guess," answered Piper, laughing it off. "I just want you all to be pleased."

CHAPTER

48

THE PROCESSIONAL HYMN WAS ALREADY playing as Terri and Vin Donovan walked into the church. They hurried halfway down the main aisle, genuflecting before they entered a pew. As the Saturday-evening Mass began, Vin was thinking of his only daughter.

For the last two days, he'd been turning to the Internet, trying to find out all he could about what was happening at Elysium. On Friday there'd been dozens of articles as newspapers around the country had run the *Los Angeles Times* front-page story. Today the *L.A. Times* had carried a much smaller piece. Vin understood, as a former cop himself, that the information provided by the police on the murder investigation was scanty. Whatever leads law enforcement had were not being shared with the press.

He took off his gloves and blew on his hands to warm

them. He said a silent prayer for Robert and Zara and the baby that was growing, cell by cell, inside his daughter-in-law. So much could go wrong. *Please, God, let my first grandchild be born strong and healthy.*

As Vin stared up at the priest, a memory flashed through his mind. Six-year-old Piper, with her front teeth missing and her veil askew, had knelt at that altar rail to receive her First Communion. How had more than two decades gone by so quickly?

He had prepared Piper as well as he knew how. Over the years he'd talked to her and explained things to her. He had tried to make her savvy so she'd know what to watch out for and always to be on guard. But try as he might, Vin couldn't cover every eventuality. At his insistence Piper had taken her karate lessons and kept mace in her purse, but at the end of the day everything couldn't be controlled or predicted.

Vin looked over at his wife. Terri had the hymnal open and was singing the second song. He wondered if she could still read the words or if she was singing from memory. The macular degeneration was a perfect example of something that had come, unbidden, and changed things. He loved Terri even more as he watched her determinedly making the adjustments to go on with her life, but he still wished she didn't have to be tested in this way.

As Vin reached out to take his wife's hand, he thought again about his daughter. Piper was like most young people. She felt invincible. Bad things might happen to others, but nothing would happen to her.

If only that could be true.

CHAPTER

49

AT PRECISELY FIVE O'CLOCK, JACK entered O'Flanagan's on Manhattan's Upper East Side. It was early to be hitting a bar, and he knew he shouldn't make a habit of it. But it was better than drinking alone in his apartment. He wanted to be around other people.

Jack had his choice of stools. He took one at the end of the bar. While he waited for the bartender to take his order, he watched the basketball game on one of the big flat-screen televisions hanging above the liquor-filled shelves.

The bartender finished wiping the counter before approaching.

"What'll it be?" he asked.

"I'll have a Guinness," said Jack.

The bartender filled a large glass with stout and put it in front of Jack. "Cheers," he said, sliding a bowl of peanuts closer to his lone customer.

Taking a swallow, Jack savored the bite of the dark brown ale. He continued to drink, thinking about Piper and what she might be doing. After hearing about the murder at Elysium, Jack had put in a call to the L.A. office and had had an agent friend there fill him in on what was happening. It was a police matter, but the agent promised to follow the situation and keep Jack apprised.

"I'll have another," said Jack, signaling to the bartender.

"You don't look happy, my friend," said the bartender as he delivered the next pint.

"I'm not," said Jack. "Woman trouble."

"What else is new?" said the bartender, leaning on the bar with his hands.

Jack shook his head. "I really think I'm in love with this girl," he said.

"Brother, I'm sorry to hear that."

In spite of himself, Jack smiled.

"Well, what's the problem?" asked the bartender.

Jack took another swallow. "She was engaged to this jackass, and he broke it off. Now she says she's afraid of getting involved again. Plus, she's an actress, and that's not going too well, so she moved back home with her parents."

"Other than that, Mrs. Lincoln, how was the play?"

"I know," said Jack, staring glumly into his glass.

"Maybe she just needs some space or has to prove she can be on her own," said the bartender. "It sounds to me like her life could use some sorting out."

"Or maybe she's just *saying* she's afraid of getting involved again. Maybe that's just an excuse. Maybe she just doesn't want to get involved with *me*."

The bartender shook his head in sympathy as the front door opened. Two men walked in and took seats at the bar.

Jack finished off his beer. "I don't know how much more I can stand," he said. "I have to talk to her."

"You do what you want, buddy," said the bartender as he turned to attend to the new customers. "But I think you should wait for her to come to you. In the meantime go out and have some fun. There are plenty of girls out there."

"I know," said Jack, remembering the young woman he'd had dinner with the night before. He had used alcohol to get through the date. With Piper he didn't need an artificial high. She turned him on stone-cold sober.

CHAPTER

50

WALKING OUT ONTO THE PATIO, Piper looked around. Only a few of the tables were occupied. She spotted Wendy Ellis sitting in the far corner.

"I hope you don't mind eating outside," said Wendy. "It's getting chilly."

Piper smiled, though she was wishing she'd brought a sweater. "Please, compared to New York, this is tropical."

"I asked them if they could bring an outdoor heater," said Wendy.

"Great," said Piper.

They scanned the menu as a waiter, dressed in a peach shirt and khaki slacks, came and filled their water glasses.

"Is it just me, or does the peach theme get to be a bit much?" Piper whispered as she watched the waiter walk away. "The soap, the candles, the golf carts, the cushions at the pool, the tablecloths—it's everywhere. You can't get away from it!"

Wendy laughed self-consciously, her hand reaching up to touch her mask. "And you've only been here a few days, right? Try staying here for weeks and weeks."

"I can only imagine what that would be like," said Piper. She waited for Wendy to expound.

"I guess it would be great if you were here just to relax and have yourself pampered," said Wendy. "But it's not so much fun when you're here like I am."

Piper wondered if she should probe further, but before she could say anything, Wendy continued.

"I guess you're probably wondering why I wear this mask."

"It's crossed my mind," answered Piper.

"I had a nose job and wasn't satisfied with it, so Dr. Abernathy did another one. That didn't come out the way I wanted either, so I had another surgery. Long story short, what's left of my nose is grotesque."

"But eventually it can be fixed, right?" asked Piper.

"I don't know," said Wendy. "Dr. Abernathy is meeting with my father and me tomorrow. We'll see what he says."

"I'm so sorry, Wendy," said Piper.

"Thanks," answered Wendy. She loosened the bottom of her mask so she could take a sip of water. "In a way I have only myself to blame. I wanted to look different, have a thinner and perfectly straight nose. Now I'd give anything to have back the one I had. I was so stupid."

Piper considered Wendy's words. She thought about all the times she'd looked in the mirror and criticized her own face or wished her stomach were flatter or her legs shaped differently, when in reality she'd been pretty lucky. Piper knew that she was too hard on herself, just like so many other women.

"I hope it goes well with Dr. Abernathy tomorrow, Wendy," she said.

"Thanks, so do I—as much for my father as for myself," said Wendy. "This whole thing has broken his heart."

CHAPTER

51

WHILE A BAG OF POPCORN popped in the microwave, Kyle pulled the drapes closed in the living room of his West Hollywood studio. He fluffed the pillows on the sofa and shook out the chenille throw gathered in a puddle on the floor. Settling in for an evening by himself, Kyle poured himself a drink, emptied the popcorn into a bowl, and stretched out on the couch.

It had been a long week, and he was exhausted, but not too tired to watch the fruits of his labors. Though there had been only one who'd agreed to the sleep treatment this week, she was an exciting one. It was always thrilling to catch a famous actress. Someday he very well might extort money from her, but for now he was content just to have his own private screening.

He clicked on the television set and made the necessary adjustments. The picture of the sleeping movie star appeared, zooming to her closed eyes and partially opened mouth. Kyle listened to his own voice narrating the video trip down her unclothed body. The camera made stops at each particularly stimulating zone. At times the video shook. Kyle smiled, remembering what he'd been doing then.

As the actress let out an unconscious moan, Kyle moaned, too. The video was over much too quickly. He played it again. And again.

Breathing heavily, he turned off the television set. He wished he had something more to watch. But none of the others he was interested in this week responded to his suggestions about the sleep treatment. One dark-haired woman had asked him about it on her own, but she wasn't his type. She had seemed very disappointed when he turned her down. Too bad she didn't meet his standards.

Kyle fleetingly considered expanding his criteria for sleep-treatment eligibility. He quickly dismissed the idea out of hand. There was no point in accepting brunettes or redheads when only blondes turned him on.

CHAPTER

52

SUNDAY, JANUARY 9 . . . SIX DAYS UNTIL
THE WEDDING

PIPER LOOKED AT THE CLOCK on the bedside table. Adding three hours, she calculated that her father would be home, making his bacon and eggs, while her mother would be at the bakery. Sunday morning was the busiest time of the week at The Icing on the Cupcake.

She picked up her cell phone and made the call. After four rings, Piper heard her mother's voice.

"Icing on the Cupcake. May I help you?"

"Hi, Mom. It's me."

"Piper, honey! How good to hear your voice. How are you?"

"Great, Mom. How are you?"

Piper could hear the sound of voices in the background. "Fine, honey. As you can imagine, it's a little hectic here."

"I know," said Piper. "I just wanted to tell you that yesterday I made your cream-cheese icing for the bride and groom and her parents, and they all flipped for it."

"Oh, I'm so glad, Piper," said Terri. "It's such a simple recipe, but sometimes the simple ones are the best. Did it go well with the pumpkin cake?"

"Actually, there were three different versions of cake," explained Piper. "The icing tasted great on all of them. But I think they're going with the original pumpkin bread. Mom, that stuff is ridiculous. It's as good as cake."

"Hold on a second, honey," said Terri. Piper could hear her answering a question posed by another voice, which Piper recognized as belonging to Cathy, her mother's BFF and right arm at the bakery. Cathy had been shouldering more work as Terri's macular degeneration had made intricate and detailed cake decorating more difficult. Knowing that Cathy was there made Piper feel better.

"Okay, where were we?" asked Terri.

"That's all right, Mom," said Piper. "You're busy. I just wanted to say hi. Tell Dad I called, and give him a kiss for me."

"Why don't you give him a call, honey? He's at home."

Piper hesitated. She knew if she called her father, he would pump her about what was going on at Elysium. He hadn't wanted her to take the job in the first place, working for a bride who the police suspected had been the target of an acid attack. Surely Esperanza's murder had him churning further. If he knew that his daughter was going to try to ensnare a suspected sexual predator, Vin would be utterly apoplectic.

If they spoke, there would be questions. Piper didn't want to lie to him. Better not to talk to him at all.

"I'm going to be totally slammed today, Mom," said Piper. "In fact, I'm late for something right now. Tell Dad I love him and I'll call him soon."

THE SOUND OF CHIRPING BIRDS filled the morning air as people gathered in the meadow to pay their respects to Esperanza Flores. Many of the mourners wore the peach uniforms of the Elysium staff. Others seemed to be guests, some of them dressed in robes, stopping to say a prayer before they went off to their spa treatments. As each person arrived, he or she was handed a helium-filled white balloon.

Piper saw Jillian clasping Ben Dixon's hand. Tears were streaming down her face. Anastasia Wilcox was standing at the periphery, her eyes darting around to take in every detail. She nodded at Piper when she saw her.

Piper also noticed that Wendy Ellis was near the back of the group. A heavyset middle-aged man was with her. Piper surmised he was Wendy's father. Knowing how hard it was for Wendy to come out in public, Piper was proud of her new friend.

At the front, Vernon and Irene Abernathy stood together. Vernon stepped forward and began to speak.

"Friends, we gather here this morning to remember Esperanza Flores. Many of you had gotten to know her well, as she lived here at Elysium over the last months. You helped her recuperate, taking good care of her as she tried to heal after the terrible agony she endured at the hands of the evil person who so viciously attacked her. To those of you who nursed Esperanza and tried to make her days as comfortable as possible, please take solace from that fact. Because of you, Esperanza knew that there are good people in this world."

Vernon's eyes scanned the audience.

"To those of you who didn't know Esperanza," he continued, "thank you for coming anyway. I know she would be touched that so many of you took the time to pay your respects when you could have been focused solely on your own pleasures.

"Esperanza's life was short and hard. But she is no longer in pain." Vernon's voice cracked. Irene grabbed hold of her husband's arm while he took a deep breath and tried to compose himself. He finally got out his final sentence.

"Here on earth we seek justice for Esperanza's death, but Esperanza herself is at peace now."

As the white balloons were released and drifted up into the sky, Piper looked around and saw several men in dark suits taking it all in, their mouths set in grim lines. She knew from TV that the police came to funerals and memorial services for murder victims, hoping that the killer would show up.

CHAPTER

53

FOLLOWING HOLY MASS AND MIDMORNING prayer, Sister Mary Noelle had a light breakfast with the other nuns in the refectory. They ate in silence, the quiet broken only by the occasional spoon scraping against the side of a cereal bowl. Afterward Sister Mary Noelle headed for the gift shop.

There would be no customers today. Sunday was the day to restock and get ready for the week ahead. The nun put on her smock and began stacking the boxes of fresh candies, displaying them to their best advantage in the glass cases. She arranged the plastic-wrapped loaves of pumpkin bread on the multitiered cart. She walked around the shop, straightening the prayer cards, religious pamphlets, and books.

Satisfied that all was as it should be, Sister Mary Noelle looked at her watch. She still had some time before midday prayer. Leaving the gift shop, she went to the convent's supply room, where she took inventory.

The drop cloths, brushes, rollers, and buckets of paint were ready and waiting for the job ahead. So was the turpentine, for any accidents that might happen.

CHAPTER

54

BEFORE THE SUN GREW TOO strong, Piper wanted to go down to the pool and get in some laps. When she got there, she was delighted to see she had the place all to herself. She sighed contentedly as she stuck her toe in at the shallow end. The water was warmer than the air temperature outside.

She swam with long, sure strokes. Back and forth, again and again. Swimming never failed to make her feel strong—both while she was doing it and afterward.

Flipping over, Piper floated, looking up at the sky and thinking. Tomorrow, first thing, she would set up an appointment for a facial with Kyle Quigley, trying to secure one for the afternoon once she got back from her audition. She made a mental note to call Anastasia and tell her that she had decided to help her find out what was going on with those suspicious sleep treatments.

The sound of iron scraping against stone roused her from her thoughts. She turned over and stood up in the water. A woman was moving a lounge chair. Blond hair protruded from beneath her big floppy hat. Though the woman was wearing sunglasses, Piper immediately recognized her.

When the woman had taken off her caftan and settled on the lounge, Piper got out of the pool. She walked past the woman and smiled.

The woman smiled back. "Have a good swim?" she asked.

"Amazing," said Piper. "Just what I needed." Her heart pounded. *And I'm talking to someone I've watched and loved since childhood!*

"It's such a great place, isn't it?" asked the actress.

Piper nodded. "Unbelievable. This is my first time here."

"Oh, well," said the actress as she covered herself with sunscreen. "I come here as much as I can. I always leave feeling so much better."

Piper hesitated for a moment before speaking. "I hope you don't mind if I tell you that I'm a big fan of yours."

The actress put her finger up to her lips. "Shh. We play a nice little game here. Everyone pretends they don't know who the guests are—and those of us who don't want the world to know that we come to Elysium for a little refreshing now and then . . . well, we appreciate no one using our names."

As the actress continued spreading the lotion on her smooth skin, Piper caught sight of an ugly and prominent black-and-blue mark on her upper thigh.

"Isn't this horrible?" asked the actress as she gently rubbed the bruise. "And the worst part is, I don't even know how I got it."

CHAPTER

55

VERNON HAD BEEN DREADING THIS day. He knew that he'd put it off as long as he could. The task ahead was so daunting that he didn't want to undertake it alone. Ben had agreed that it would be a good idea if he came along to offer support to everyone involved.

The men stood at the cottage door, looking at each other, and then both of them drew a deep breath before Vernon knocked. George Ellis opened the door. His expression was solemn.

"Good morning, gentlemen," he said. "Come in."

The two doctors entered and took seats in the chairs across from the sofa where Wendy was waiting. George sat next to his daughter and grabbed her hand.

"How are you, Wendy?" asked Dr. Ben.

"You're going to be so proud of me," she said. "I did what you wanted me to do. I talked to someone new on Friday after I left your office, and yesterday I had dinner with her." Wendy paused for effect. "On the patio!"

Dr. Ben smiled broadly. "Good for you, Wendy! That's wonderful."

"Yeah, it was great," said Wendy. "Piper's going to be here all week. I think we'll see each other again."

"That must be Piper Donovan, I'm guessing," said Dr. Abernathy.

"Yes," said Wendy, nodding enthusiastically. "That's right. You know her. She's making your daughter's wedding cake." She turned to Dr. Ben. "That's your wedding cake, too."

"Right," said Dr. Ben. He looked over at his future father-in-law. Vernon cleared his throat.

"Do you need some water, Dr. Abernathy?" asked Wendy.

Her father spoke before Vernon could answer. "I think Dr. Abernathy has something he wants to tell us, Wendy. Don't you, Doctor?"

Vernon shifted uncomfortably in his chair. "Yes, I'm afraid I do."

Wendy looked from man to man, her eyes widening as she sensed that something bad was coming.

Vernon continued, deliberately softening his tone. "Wendy, I think the time has come for us to face the fact that there is nothing to be done. We aren't going to be able to correct things."

"Ever?" Wendy asked in barely a whisper.

"Not now," said Vernon. "Not with the capabilities we currently have. In time there may be new techniques developed. We can hope that in the future there will be a way we can rebuild your nose. But for now the best and only option is a prosthetic."

"You mean this hole in my face will still be here?" Wendy cried. "You want me to have a nose that I put on and take off?"

"One can be made that will look so good that no one will know it isn't real," said Vernon.

"*I'll* know!" yelled Wendy. She turned to her father and threw her arms around his neck. As she sobbed, his face reddened. George held her, patting her hair. There were tears in his own eyes.

"I think that's all for now, gentlemen," he managed to say.

"If you need me, Wendy, if you want to talk," said Dr. Ben, "I'll be available through the switchboard."

The doctors got up and left. George stayed behind and tried to soothe his devastated child.

CHAPTER

56

FOR THE FIRST TIME IN a long time, Hudson was going to drive through the *front* gate. He smiled at the security guard, not recognizing his face. Hudson briefly wondered how many other new hires had been made since he'd been the director.

"I'm Hudson Sherwood. I have an appointment with Dr. Abernathy."

The guard consulted his clipboard. "Yes, Mr. Sherwood. Dr. Abernathy is waiting for you at his home. You go down this road—"

Hudson interrupted. "I know where it is."

"Yes, sir," said the guard as he pushed the button to raise the gate.

Driving away, Hudson took it as a good sign that Vernon

had agreed to meet with him so quickly when he'd called the doctor yesterday. An even better sign was that Vernon had invited him to have lunch. That signaled that he was allotting at least an hour for them to talk.

Hudson was determined to be pleasant and not show any animosity. Vernon's decision to have Jillian replace him as Elysium's director had caused Hudson years of misery, but this wasn't the time to rehash all that. Vernon had to think that Hudson wanted to let bygones be bygones, even if he didn't really feel that way at all.

As his car pulled into the Abernathys' driveway, Hudson's hands gripped the steering wheel so hard that his knuckles were white. He stared at the sprawling house on the well-tended grounds. Vernon Abernathy had been living large while Hudson Sherwood had been reduced to clipping coupons out of the newspaper to save a few cents on toilet paper.

He turned off the ignition and glanced in the rearview mirror. *Wipe that scowl off your face, you idiot. He's never going to rehire you if you look like you want to kill somebody.*

CHAPTER

57

WHEN SHE GOT TO HER room, Piper sat on the bed, took a deep breath, and called Anastasia.

"All right," she told the reporter. "I'm in."

"Really? That's fantastic, Piper. Thank you," said Anastasia. "Maybe we should get together, talk over the details, and come up with a more precise plan. Want to meet at the pool?"

"I was just down there," said Piper. "And guess who I saw?"

Anastasia chuckled. "Let me think. Was it a blond actress who hasn't done anything in a long time?"

"How'd you know?"

"Because I was excited the first time I spotted her, too. Plus, I saw her this morning with her beach bag and caftan. I knew where she was headed."

CHAPTER

58

As George watched his daughter, he was deeply relieved. She had finally fallen asleep. Wendy had cried for so long—deep, racking sobs that tore at him. As much as he tried, George couldn't console her. Gradually, though, the tears subsided and Wendy just stared straight ahead for what felt like forever, saying nothing. Finally she got up from the sofa, went to her bed, and lay down.

She closed her eyes and murmured, "I don't want to live anymore."

"Oh, angel, it seems like that now," George said softly as he sat on the edge of the mattress. "But you'll see. It will work out."

Wendy opened her eyes above the mask. "No it won't," she said. "But I love you, Dad."

"I love you, too, sweetheart."

He listened for her breathing to become deeper and more even. Once he was satisfied that Wendy was truly asleep, he returned to the living room. Exhausted by physical and mental fatigue, he kicked off his shoes, put his feet up on the sofa, and lay back.

The phone rang. George grabbed the receiver before it could ring a second time, lifting it and hanging it up again. Then he set it to not ring.

Deep as his anger was, he was too tired to scream or yell or lash out in despair. What good would that do anyway? There was no point in holding his fist up to God and chastising him for the tragedy that had caused, and would continue to cause, Wendy the most dreadful anguish. God wasn't to blame.

Vernon Abernathy was.

CHAPTER

59

THE BLOND ACTRESS WAS JUST getting up from her chaise when Piper and Anastasia arrived at the pool area. Piper nudged her companion and led the way to chairs just past where the actress had been lounging.

"Hello again," said Piper as they walked by.

The actress smiled sweetly. "Back so soon?"

"I wanted to keep my friend company," said Piper.

The actress stretched. "Well, I'm going to head upstairs and take a nap. I don't know why I'm so tired. I had the most wonderful sleep treatment yesterday. You'd think I'd be totally rested."

Piper and Anastasia looked at each other.

"Oh, really?" asked Anastasia. "What's that like?"

"They have a wonderful paramedical aesthetician here,"

said the actress as she stuffed a magazine into her bag. "His name is Kyle. I went for a facial, and he suggested this new treatment he's developed. He said they're doing it in Europe but not in the United States yet, except for him."

"I haven't seen any sleep treatment on the spa menu," said Piper.

"That's why," said the actress. "It needs FDA approval or something. I guess because he gives you an injection."

"Of what?" asked Anastasia.

"I don't really know," said the actress. "I saw the bottle, and it looked very official, but I didn't really notice the name of the stuff. Besides, I wouldn't worry. A place like Elysium wouldn't do anything that wasn't safe."

Slipping on her sandals, the actress started to pull her caftan over her head. Piper elbowed Anastasia and nodded in the direction of the actress's long, slender legs. Anastasia looked in time to see the giant bruise on the right thigh.

"Whatever Kyle did, I'm going back for more," said the actress, gathering up the rest of her things. "My face hasn't looked or felt this good in ages."

CHAPTER

60

W ELL, THANK YOU FOR LUNCH, Irene," said Hudson as he
rose from his chair. "That was the best chicken salad."

"I wish I could take credit for it," said Irene, smiling and touching her expertly tinted hair. "But I had them bring it over from the Elysium kitchen. Just think: You'll be having that food again all the time."

"I'll be looking forward to that," said Hudson. He glanced at his watch. "I can't believe how late it is. I've been here for almost three hours."

"Time well spent," said Vernon as he patted Hudson on the shoulder. "I'm so glad we're both willing to let bygones be bygones. It will be good to have you with us again, Hudson. I know that Jillian feels the same way. She's well aware that she needs help. And after the wedding I want her to take some time off, even after she and Ben come home from their honeymoon. So I'm glad you can start right away."

"Yes," said Irene, slipping her arm through her husband's and snuggling against him. "Vernon has been so worried about Jillian. All of us will rest easier having you as Elysium's assistant director."

Hudson's jaw tensed. He managed to smile, shake hands with Vernon, and kiss Irene on the cheek. As he walked out to his car, Irene's words irked him. Assistant director wasn't good enough.

CHAPTER

61

THE CLOISTERED SISTERS AT THE Monastery of the Angels looked forward to the second Sunday of every month, a day of fewer chores and a more relaxed, retreatlike schedule. Today the bells rang at two forty-five so that the sisters would be gathered in the chapel by three o'clock for the special speaker.

Mother never revealed who the visitor would be, so it was a surprise to watch a Passionist monk leave his pew and walk toward a wooden lectern set up in front of the altar. The light that illuminated the golden tabernacle also took in the lectern. The tall, handsome, black-haired priest stepped into the glow.

Sister Mary Noelle took the measure of the man. Crisp black cassock, with a heart-shaped emblem sewn over his chest. His left hand was wrapped around a foot-high wooden crucifix stuffed into the wide black leather belt around his waist. He was the spitting image of Gregory Peck—as if he had just stepped off the set of *To Kill a Mockingbird*. She thought, *This is going to be good.*

"My dear sisters," he began, "God wants one thing, and one thing only, from each and every one of you." He shifted the crucifix from its jaunty position over his left hip to a spot perpendicular to his ribs, his fingers enclosing the shoulders and chest of the dead Christ. "He wants something beautiful."

He looked out at the nuns, most of whom were middle-aged and elderly. He paused before continuing to speak.

"Many of us in this chapel can remember, over forty years ago, the documentary on Mother Teresa called *Something Beautiful for God*. The journalist in the documentary believed that a miracle had taken place during the filming. Technicians had predicted that there wasn't enough light to shoot the scenes in the Home for the Dying. But when they viewed the processed film, those scenes were bathed in a beautiful, soft light.

"It may shock some of you to hear me tell a rather brutal truth: Mother Teresa was not a pretty woman, by earthly standards. In fact, the week she died, one of the most beautiful women in the world had also died. Princess Diana's funeral shifted the attention of the world to her and left television commentators with the unenviable task of trying to make comparisons."

The priest moved away from the podium, walked down the center aisle, and stood in the midst of the sisters. Every eye was on him—and the nuns sitting in the front pews had to turn around in order to see him.

"Both women, they said, had devoted their lives to charitable causes. Both women had experienced sadness and had overcome obstacles. And both women, they said, were known throughout the whole world. But the one comparison they could not make—dared not make—was that they were both beautiful. Simply because one of them was the most photographed woman in the world, one who set off a new fashion trend whenever she left her palace. And the other? She was a gnarled, wrinkled, hunched-over gnome of a creature who set fashion back a hundred years every time she stooped to pick up a dying man from the gutters of India.

"No one can deny that Princess Diana captured the world's attention with her daring work for land-mine victims and the compassion that moved her to hold children dying of AIDS in her arms. In fact, it was not only her royalty but also her God-given and astonishing beauty that made her charitable work possible.

"However, I ask you, sisters: Was Blessed Teresa of Calcutta any less beautiful?" The preacher gripped the crucifix one last time and raised his voice. "The answer to that question is what convinces me that I know what the Lord desires. He wants each of you—no matter how the outside world judges such things—he wants each of you to be 'something beautiful for God.'

"Don't disappoint him."

All the sisters remained in the chapel long after the preacher left, considering his words.

Sister Mary Noelle knelt in prayer. She certainly did not want to disappoint God. As she buried her face in her hands, she prayed, *Lord, will nothing convince my sister Jillian to stop wasting her life on wrinkle creams and tummy tucks—and, like Princess Diana, start using her beauty for good?*

CHAPTER

62

MONDAY, JANUARY 10 . . . FIVE DAYS UNTIL
THE WEDDING

THE DISTANCE FROM ELYSIUM TO where Piper's audition
would take place was only eleven miles, but it took her
almost an hour to get there. Cars and vans inched along
Santa Monica Boulevard. From the rear seat of the car, Piper
noted that virtually none of the other vehicles carried more
than one passenger.

Piper had heard about the misery of Los Angeles traffic.
After living in and commuting to Manhattan, she'd always
dismissed the stories as West Coast whining. It had never oc-
curred to her that anything was worse than the FDR at rush
hour. Now she felt as if she should draft a letter of apology to

all the residents of Los Angeles County. It truly was different here. Like the sunshine, traffic was a given.

While it was worse during rush hours, it rarely seemed to relent. Piper had taken her newfound understanding into account when she'd booked her driver. The thought of being late for an audition made her heart race. She was well aware that being stressed rarely led to a booking.

She wanted this one. Big-time. A national dog-food commercial had the potential of providing residuals checks for months and months to come. Piper still got an occasional check from the shampoo commercial she'd done a couple of years ago. At this point she would welcome any income.

More than the money, though, she just needed to book something. Except for the episodes of the soap *A Little Rain Must Fall* that she'd done in December, Piper had not worked in months. She knew that Gabe had faith in her, but some days it felt like she'd lost faith in herself. Gabe always tried to reassure her. "Doll, one day it'll start to rain, and then it will pour," he'd tell her. Piper laughed to herself at the irony of looking for career precipitation in arid Los Angeles.

"This shouldn't take too long," she said to the driver as she got out of the car. She walked up the path and entered the building, which had been converted from a house to a place of business, then signed in at the desk in the front hall.

She picked up a storyboard sheet as she took a seat in the waiting room. The sheet was divided into four squares. The first showed a man and a nervous woman standing at the front door of a house; the second showed the door being opened by an older man and woman; and the third showed the younger, nervous woman now smiling as she leaned over to pet a dog. In the final square, all four people and the dog seemed thrilled to be together.

Piper glanced around the waiting room. Two good-looking guys stood chatting just inside the door. Three other girls had gotten there before her. Just like Piper, all three were blondes. A few moments later, a brunette with a clipboard came into the room.

"Piper? Tom?" She didn't even look up as she called their names. Piper and the taller of the two guys walked into the audition room. The girl with the clipboard settled behind a camera that had been set up on a tripod. Next to the camera was a foldout table with a man sitting on the other side of it. He looked to be about forty and had a deep tan that complemented his short, sandy blond hair. A phone book rested on a folding chair in front of the table.

"Piper, Tom, welcome," said the casting director. "So here's what we've got: An engaged couple goes to see the guy's parents. The girl is nervous to be meeting her soon-to-be in-laws for the first time. The parents and their dog answer the door. The girl makes friends with the dog, causing the parents to like her immediately. Everyone's happy. So what I'll have you do is slate your name and height, and then we can go into a little improvisation of the scenario. You can use me as the parents, and, Piper, you use the phone book on the chair as the dog. Okay? Great."

Piper looked at Tom, her new boyfriend. He smiled and

wordlessly gestured, *Ladies first*. Piper looked into the camera lens and said, "Hi, I'm Piper Donovan, and I'm five-eight."

Tom immediately followed with "And I'm Tom Glass, five-eleven."

Piper turned to Tom and started to say something about how nervous she was to meet his parents when Tom grabbed her shoulders and started screaming in her face, "You can do this! They're just my parents. Don't let them break you!"

Piper instantly went with it. "I won't! I won't!" she cried as her face broke into the beginning of a sob. In unison, Piper and Tom whipped around to face the casting director.

"Mom! Dad!" Tom extended his arms for a big hug.

"Hi . . . uh, Mom? Dad?" Piper whimpered. Then she directed her attention to the phone book, and her eyes lit up. She breathed in and clapped her hands together as a smile spread across her face. "Oh, look, how cute you are! Hello there, little doggy. Why are you so cute?"

Piper picked up the phone book and cradled it in her arms. She brought the book with her as she made her way back to stand next to a now-grinning Tom. He wrapped his arm around her and beamed at the casting director. Piper matched his glow and with total confidence repeated the words of her initial greeting: "Hi, Mom. Dad." She nuzzled the phone book as she heard the casting director burst out laughing.

"Wow, guys. That was really fun," he said, still laughing.

Piper looked over at the girl behind the camera, and even she was giggling.

The casting director continued, "Okay, thank you so much for coming in, great meeting you guys, and we'll be in touch."

Piper and Tom thanked him for his time and walked from the room, through the waiting area, and out the door. As they were about to turn in separate directions, Tom extended his hand. Piper smiled as she took it.

"Well, I'll see you at the callback, Piper Donovan," he said.

"Hope so, Tom."

As she turned toward her car, Piper hadn't felt so good about an audition in at least a year. It was as if all the acting anxiety she'd had in New York had been melted by the California sunshine.

CHAPTER

63

TWO GLASS BOTTLES SAT ON *the bench along with a funnel,* *rags, a gallon of turpentine, a can of motor oil, and a container of liquid soap. The peach-gloved hands inserted the funnel into the neck and carefully poured the turpentine halfway up the first bottle. Then the process was repeated.*

Next, motor oil and liquid soap were added to both bottles. The soap would help the burning liquid adhere to the target, while the oil would create clouds of thick, choking smoke. If the fire wasn't fatal, maybe smoke inhalation would do the trick.

The rags were dropped into a bucket and doused with the remaining turpentine. When the time came, the soaked cloths would be stuffed into the bottle necks, each serving as a wick leading down to the flammable liquid.

The bottles and bucket were placed in an airtight cooler and then stashed where nobody would come upon them. The empty cans of motor oil and turpentine were tossed. There was quite a bit of liquid soap left in the container. It was silly to throw that away. Waste not, want not.

When the time was right, when it was possible to do it without being seen, when the lights were all out at the cottage and the inhabitant was sound asleep, the simple firebombs would be assembled, lit, and hurled at the target.

CHAPTER

64

AFTER VERNON LEFT FOR HIS office in the main building, Irene put five miles in on her exercise bike. She showered, dressed, and applied her makeup. Then she made two phone calls. The second one was to her stepdaughter.

"I just got off the phone with Kyle," she announced. "I've booked us back-to-back facials with him this afternoon," Irene announced.

"Oh, I don't know, Irene," answered Jillian. "I have so much to do around here."

"Let Hudson take care of things for a couple of hours. That's what he's there for. To help you."

"I know, but it's his first day back."

"He'll be fine," said Irene. "Your wedding is only five

days away, Jillian. You should have the facial today, so any redness afterward will be gone by Saturday."

There was silence for a moment as Jillian considered her stepmother's proposal. "You know, you're right, Irene," said Jillian. "I'm getting married, and even though I feel absolutely terrible about Esperanza, I should try to enjoy this time."

"Exactly," said Irene. "Moping around isn't going to bring Esperanza back."

She instantly regretted her choice of words. "I didn't mean you've been moping, dear," she said.

"That's all right, Irene," said Jillian. "I know what you meant. I *have* been dragging around. But I'm glad that I have you to talk straight to me and pull me out of it."

"Good," said Irene. "So we're on with our facials?"

"Yes. We're on," said Jillian. "And do you want to see if Dad wants to meet us for lunch first?"

"Sure," said Irene. "I know there's nothing your father would enjoy more. He always lights up when you're around."

CHAPTER

65

PIPER CAME OUT OF THE audition feeling jubilant. She knew she'd done well. Now she had to wait to hear from Gabe. He would follow up with the casting director for feedback.

When she was in the car again, Piper took out her phone and updated her Facebook status:

FUN AUDITION THIS MORNING!
KEEP YOUR FINGERS CROSSED FOR ME!

As the car traveled east on Santa Monica Boulevard, Piper's stomach growled. She watched out the window for a place to get a little something to eat. The sign for The Butter End Cakery came into view. It was worth a shot.

"Hey, pull over here," she said on impulse. "I'll run in and get something for us. Any preferences?"

"Whatever looks good," said the driver, shifting the car into park. "I like just about everything."

"Me, too," said Piper as she got out. "I'll be right back." She waited for a chance to run across the busy road.

The Butter End was part bakery, part industrial storage, part school. The large space, with its high ceilings and unfinished walls, was divided into sections. Upstairs there was an open loft, stacked with bags of baking materials and equipment. Below, a long, stainless-steel counter lined with bar stools separated the entrance from the kitchen on the other side. Professional refrigerators and ovens were plainly visible. A woman was rolling out fondant icing on the kitchen worktable. She glanced up and smiled when Piper cleared her throat.

"Hi, I'm Kimberly." The woman looked at her watch. "If you're here for a lesson, you're early."

"Actually, I'm here to get something to eat," said Piper.

"I just made some scones for the class," said Kimberly, putting down the rolling pin. "Apricot and currant."

"Sounds good," said Piper. "How about one of each?"

Kimberly took the clear dome off a metal cake stand. As the baker selected the scones, Piper looked around.

"So you give baking lessons here?" she asked.

"Yes," said Kimberly. "Twice a week. But most of my business is specialty work. Cakes for birthdays, graduations, anniversaries, charity events, weddings. You name it. There's a book of pictures of some of the cakes if you want to take a look." She nodded to the scrapbook sitting on the corner of the counter.

Piper flipped though the plastic-covered pages. The variety of cakes and their execution were both impressive. A teddy bear, an L.A. Dodgers baseball cap, a dinosaur, a spider, a sports car, a soccer ball, a basketball, book covers, even a cake that looked like a hamburger and another that was fashioned after a toilet. The multitiered wedding cakes were breathtaking. Kimberly obviously had special skill for creating the most beautiful frosting flowers.

"Wow, this butterfly looks like it could up and fly away," said Piper, pointing to one of the pictures. "You're really talented."

"Thanks," said Kimberly. "I try."

As Piper left the shop with her warm scones, she wondered if Jillian or Irene knew about The Butter End. She hoped not. This Kimberly chick was a force. Piper knew that it was time to focus on the reason she'd been brought out here. She wanted to make a cake good enough to ensure that Jillian would never regret the decision to hire her.

CHAPTER

66

D R. BEN DIXON WAS WHISTLING as he turned the corner of the hallway. He stopped abruptly when he spotted George Ellis waiting at the door to Ben's office. George's facial expression was dour, his complexion gray. He wore a rumpled sport shirt, the same one he had on the day before. It stretched over a sizable gut.

The poor guy is a good candidate for a heart attack, thought Ben as he smiled at George.

"I know I don't have an appointment, Doc," said George. "But I feel like I have to talk or I'll burst."

"Of course, George. I have a half hour before my first patient. Will that be enough time?"

"It has to be, I guess," said George.

Ben unlocked the office door and stood aside so George

could enter first. Taking a chair across the desk from Ben, George sat with his fists clenched.

"It was hard news to hear yesterday," said Ben.

"The worst."

"How did Wendy do after Vernon and I left?"

"She cried and cried and cried until she fell asleep. I stayed overnight in the cottage with her. I was afraid to leave her."

"You've been a rock for her through all of this, George. Wendy loves you very much."

George sighed. "It's been just Wendy and me for a long time. When her mother took off, I tried to fill that role, too."

"It can't have been easy," said Ben.

"No, I guess not," George said quietly. "I haven't always done the best job."

"Why do you say that?"

"Because I shouldn't have allowed Wendy to have the very first surgery," said George, his eyes watering, "but she wanted it so badly that I gave in. I just wanted to make her happy, but instead I've ruined her life."

He bent forward, put his elbows on his knees, and covered his eyes.

"Wendy is over eighteen, George," said Ben softly. "She had the surgery as an adult. It was her decision. You are not to blame."

George looked up. "And she is?" he asked, incredulous. "That's just wrong. She was too young to know the chance she was taking."

"Not legally," said Ben.

"You think I care about what's legal?" George bellowed. "She's my daughter, for God's sake, and I should have protected her!"

"All right, George," said Ben, trying to calm him. "You think you didn't fight Wendy hard enough because you loved her and wanted to make her happy. Wendy was determined to have the surgery, an operation that she had every right to decide she wanted. Neither of you went into this thinking that it would turn out so poorly. You have to try to stop beating yourself up and looking to assign blame. You're not responsible for what happened. Neither is Wendy. Sometimes things just don't work out, and it's nobody's fault."

George listened silently. It was easy for Ben Dixon to say. You could tell, just by looking at him, that everything had always worked out for him. He didn't know what it was like to watch the destruction of the life of somebody he loved.

CHAPTER

67

FROM THE CAR PIPER CALLED Elysium and asked to be put through to the skin-care center. She was informed that the only appointment Kyle had left that day was at four o'clock. She booked it.

Next she called Anastasia.

"Hey, it's Piper. I'm getting the facial."

"Perfect," said Anastasia. "I was thinking that it would be great to have video of all this. It would give us evidence of how he proposes the treatments to his victims. How would you feel about bringing a camera?"

"I don't know," Piper said, mindful that the driver could hear everything she said. "That might be more than I can handle."

"We'll install it in your purse," said Anastasia. "You can start it recording before you go into the treatment room. All you have to do is put your bag on the counter and point it toward the table."

It sounded easy enough.

CHAPTER

68

IT WAS HARD TO BE in the same room with Jillian. To spend the morning taking directions from someone young enough to be his daughter annoyed him. To take directions from the person who'd stolen his job made Hudson angry.

He was beyond thrilled when Jillian told him she was leaving for lunch with her father and stepmother and was then going for a facial. She wouldn't be back until midafternoon.

"I hope you don't mind, Hudson," said Jillian. "I hope you don't think I'm deserting you on your first day."

Hudson forced a smile. "Of course not, Jillian. I'll be absolutely fine. Don't forget, I'm not exactly a stranger to this place."

When she left for lunch, Hudson went to her desk. Jillian

was a fastidious little thing. Except for the phone and appointment book, her desktop was clear. He flipped through
the pages. Jillian and Ben were having dinner tonight. Tomorrow night was clear, and there were few notations for the
rest of the week. Other than a couple of day appointments,
Jillian hadn't scheduled anything for the week leading up to
her wedding.

Hudson sat behind the desk. It had once been his desk. It
would be his desk again.

CHAPTER

69

WHEN THE CAR DROPPED HER off in Elysium's courtyard, it was lunchtime. Piper decided not to return to her room. Instead she walked down to Wendy's cottage and knocked.

"Who is it?" Wendy asked from the other side of the door.

"It's Piper. I wanted to see if you were in the mood to have lunch."

The door opened a crack. "I'm sorry, Piper, I don't really feel like seeing anybody right now."

"Are you all right, Wendy? I called you a couple of times, but nobody answered."

"I know. I was here, but I just couldn't pick up the phone."

"Is there anything I can do to help?" Piper asked gently.

"Yes, if you can make me a new nose." Wendy opened the door wider. Piper could see she'd been crying.

"Dr. Abernathy told me there's nothing else he can do," Wendy continued. "So that's it."

"Oh, man, I'm so, so sorry," said Piper. "I know that Dr. Abernathy is great and everything, but maybe another doctor could do something. Have you thought about getting a second opinion?"

Wendy shook her head. "Maybe someday I will, but right now the thought of getting my hopes up just to have them shattered again is more than I can take. I don't think my father can take any more either. He's beside himself."

CHAPTER

70

WHAT A PRODUCTIVE DAY IT had been!
This morning the actress had come for her second sleep treatment. Kyle was confident that the video he'd taken was going to be extremely exciting to watch. Almost as exciting as it had been to record. When she woke up, the actress had been so happy with the way her skin glowed that she was eager to schedule a third treatment.

As long as women were obsessed with their appearance, he would have takers for his sleep treatments. It didn't really matter if his clients actually looked better afterward or not. They *wanted* to look better, and therefore almost all of them *believed* they looked better after treatment.

Of course, when Irene and Jillian Abernathy had come in for their facials, he hadn't suggested the sleep treatment to them, even though they both met the "blond" criterion. Irene, though a little too old for his liking, still looked good. And Jillian . . . well, Jillian was gorgeous. But it would be stupid to take a chance with them.

Still, it had been fun to massage the lotions into Jillian's flawless skin, slowly stroking her face, working down her neck, and traveling down her long, slim arms. He'd rubbed and massaged her hands with cream, imagining what it would be like to have her hold him with them. He'd gotten into such a state that he almost hadn't been able to shake himself back to reality.

As far as Jillian was concerned, he was an employee, nothing more. As much as he wished it were otherwise, that's the way it was. It wasn't going to change. Ben Dixon was a lucky SOB.

Kyle spread fresh linen on the massage table. He had one more appointment for the day. He hoped she was a blonde.

CHAPTER

71

ANASTASIA HAD ASKED PIPER TO come to her room to learn how to operate the small video camera.

"It's easy. You just push this and it will start recording," she said, pointing to the RECORD button.

"I think I can handle that," said Piper. Her outward confidence belied the doubt she was beginning to feel. If Kyle Quigley really was doing what Anastasia thought he was, he could be dangerous if he felt threatened.

"Just go in there and act as you would when going for any facial," said Anastasia. "The camera will do all the work. When he brings up the sleep treatment, try to get him to talk about it as much as possible."

Piper took the camera from Anastasia. "Okay, how do I install this in my purse?" she asked.

"I've been thinking about that," said Anastasia. "No point in putting a hole in your bag. Use mine. It's camera-ready."

Piper pulled her wallet and room key card from her purse and transferred them to Anastasia's black leather hobo bag. She wished she had the small spray can of mace that she'd promised her father she'd carry, but it had been confiscated by airline security in Newark.

Her father. Piper tried to push him out of her mind. She didn't even want to consider how he would react when he learned what she was doing. Jack either. But when she told them—*if* she told them—the meeting with Kyle Quigley would be in the past.

AFTER CHANGING INTO A PEACH-COLORED smock given to her by one of the attendants in the skin-care center, Piper settled down in the waiting area outside Kyle's treatment room. She picked up a magazine and paged through it, but she couldn't concentrate.

"Piper?"

She looked up at the powerfully built man standing in the doorway. "Yes?"

"Hi. I'm Kyle. Come on in."

As she rose from her chair, Piper suddenly realized she'd forgotten to turn on the video camera. She felt her pulse quicken and her face begin to grow hot. *Idiot. What are you going to do now?*

She followed Kyle into the treatment room. *Stay calm*, she told herself. *Stay calm.*

"Is everything all right, Piper?" asked Kyle. "You look worried. This isn't going to hurt a bit, you know."

"Oh, no. I'm fine." She managed to smile. "I was just thinking about something else."

Kyle gestured to the table. "Climb up and we'll get started."

Think of something. Now.

As she approached the table, she began to cough. "Hold on a sec," she said. "Let me get something to suck on."

With her back to Kyle, blocking his view of what she was doing, Piper put Anastasia's bag on the counter, pointing the end of it, where the opening was, at the massage table. She reached into the bag and felt the camera. Now she had to hit the RECORD button.

"Sorry. I can't find a thing in this purse," she said, stalling.

"Not to worry," said Kyle. "You're my last appointment for the day. I don't have any pressure about time."

Her fingers groped over the surface of the camera. She felt the button and pushed.

"Okay, all set," said Piper, turning around. She climbed up and lay on the table. Kyle switched on a bright light and positioned it over her face.

"So what do you do, Piper?"

"Well, on the good days, I act," she said, pretending to be sucking on a lozenge.

Kyle smiled. "As you probably know, we get a lot of actresses here."

"I know," said Piper. She deliberately didn't mention the name of the actress at the pool. "But I came here because I was asked to make Jillian Abernathy's wedding cake."

"I'm confused," said Kyle. "I thought you said you were an actress."

"I am," said Piper. "But let's just say there's a lot of downtime between acting gigs." She faked a cough.

He finished studying her pores. "Your skin looks great, Piper," he said. "There's virtually no sun damage."

"Thanks. That's because I hate to go out in it."

"I wish everyone felt that way," said Kyle as he pushed aside the lamp. "So many people come in here after they've ruined their skin by baking in the sun. Then they want me to wave a magic wand and make it disappear."

"Well, I have heard you can perform miracles," said Piper.

Kyle smiled. "Oh, yeah? Where did you hear that?"

"I was talking to someone at the pool. She was raving about some sort of sleep treatments you give."

Kyle reached for a container of cleansing cream. He scooped some out and smoothed it all over Piper's face and neck.

"That feels great," she said, completely creeped out. "You have such a nice touch."

"We'll just leave this on for a minute or two," said Kyle. "To give it time to dissolve dirt and oils." He returned the cap to its container.

"Can you tell me about the sleep treatment?" asked Piper. "Would there be a benefit for me?"

"You don't really need one, Piper," answered Kyle. "Your skin is flawless."

"Really?" asked Piper. "I'm only twenty-seven, but look at those lines at the corners of my eyes."

Kyle looked. "You've got to be kidding," he said. "There's nothing there. You don't need a sleep treatment."

That wasn't at all the answer Piper expected.

She left the center with smooth, clear skin and a case of utter confusion. Was Anastasia wrong? Was Kyle just what he appeared to be? Was he a well-trained and talented medical aesthetician with nothing to hide?

Anastasia was supposed to meet Piper for dinner. She was going to be disappointed when she heard that Kyle hadn't suggested the sleep treatments. In fact, he'd adamantly said that Piper wasn't a candidate. Maybe Anastasia's friend had been wrong in her suspicions. Maybe the black-and-blue mark on the movie star's leg had been the result of her bumping into something and she simply didn't remember. Maybe Anastasia was chasing a story that didn't exist.

CHAPTER

72

JACK COULDN'T KEEP HIMSELF FROM checking Piper's Facebook page.

FUN AUDITION THIS MORNING!

KEEP YOUR FINGERS CROSSED FOR ME!

Normally, if Jack read that post, he would have picked up the phone right away and called her. He loved sharing her happy news of any acting success. He also loved being there for her when the acting breaks weren't coming her way. Bottom line? Good or bad, he loved her.

While he had taken the bartender's advice, hanging

tough and not calling her, Jack didn't feel all that trium-
phant. Instead he just felt disappointed and worried that she
hadn't called him either.

One of them was going to have to be the bigger person
and make the first move. Jack was almost ready to cave.

CHAPTER

73

AFTER THROWING THE USED SHEETS and towels into the laundry bin and making up the massage table for the next day, Kyle went to the cabinet. Concealed by lotion bottles, his camera sat on the shelf with its eye exposed. It was trained on the table. He took it down, picked out the disc, and inserted another before replacing the camera in its hiding spot.

The moment Kyle had seen the bag Piper was carrying, he knew he'd seen it before. That Anastasia Wilcox who came in last week asking about the sleep treatment, the one with the short, dark hair whom he'd told she wasn't a candidate, had the same bag—black leather with a purple drawstring. At first Kyle wrote it off to coincidence. Many women owned the same purse. Manufacturers made hundreds of them.

But when Piper asked about the sleep treatment, he became alarmed. She had flawless skin. Even though Kyle knew from experience that many women asked for treatments they didn't need, Piper's request was ludicrous.

Maybe he was wrong. But he had learned to trust his instincts. His gut told him that something wasn't right. It had killed him not to encourage Piper to take the treatment. Young, blond, and beautiful, she was the perfect embodiment of his desires. But he couldn't take the chance.

What if Piper Donovan and the Wilcox woman were trying to trap him? What if they suspected what he'd been doing and were trying to catch him in the act? If he was found out, the professional reputation he'd worked so hard to establish would be ruined. Even worse, he'd face a stiff prison sentence.

He had to find out what was going on.

CHAPTER

74

TUESDAY, JANUARY 11 . . . FOUR DAYS UNTIL
THE WEDDING

PIPER HAD A HEADACHE. SHE and Anastasia had ordered
martinis, and afterward they'd shared a bottle of wine
and finished with amaretto cordials. Even as she drank,
Piper knew she would pay for it in the morning. And right
on cue, the dull throb began as soon as she opened her eyes.

She swallowed some ibuprofen along with a glass of
water, then lay back on the bed and closed her eyes. Her
mind went over what had happened—or not happened—in
Kyle Quigley's massage room.

Anastasia had been disappointed when she heard Piper's

account of what Kyle had said and done when Piper lay on the massage table. But she wasn't deterred in her belief that Kyle was doing something disgustingly wrong. She said she had another way she was going to try to go at him.

Rolling over onto her stomach, Piper was glad to be out of the whole thing. She'd helped Anastasia as much as she could. Now she had to get in gear on the wedding cake. The layers could be made by the nuns on Thursday, and she would then decorate the cake the following day so all would be perfect for the Saturday wedding.

Piper was thrilled that Jillian didn't want peach-colored flowers. She preferred an all-white cake, on the outside at least. The couple had decided they wanted to go with the original dense pumpkin-bread recipe for their cake. One, it tasted delicious. Two, they were planning to put little cards at each place setting explaining the story of the cloistered convent and its dependence on the sale of its pumpkin bread for survival. They hoped to increase awareness that would spur sales after the wedding.

Piper was sketching the flowers for the cake when her phone rang. She looked down at the lit-up BlackBerry. It was Gabe.

"Hey, doll, good news. They loved you at the audition yesterday. They want you to come for a callback this afternoon. If you get it, they're planning to shoot on Thursday or Friday."

"Thursday or Friday *this* week?" asked Piper, thinking about the wedding cake that had to be decorated on Friday.

"Yeah, kid. Isn't that great?" The agent didn't wait for Piper's answer. "It looks like something could be breaking for you."

CHAPTER

75

THE PHONE CALL WAS SOBERING. Anastasia's editor told her that she should be ready to pack up and leave Elysium at any time.

"Vernon Abernathy is on the warpath, Anastasia. Our publisher is a golf buddy of his, and Abernathy has been demanding to know who Anastasia Fernands is."

"He didn't tell him, did he?" she asked.

"No, but Abernathy is in a rage about those pictures you took. He says his lawyers tell him he can sue us, because there's a no-cameras policy at Elysium."

"*Can* he sue?" asked Anastasia.

"Of course. This is America. I guess his lawyers can do anything they want. Whether they'd win or not is another story. The point is, you should know that your time at Elysium is almost over and act accordingly."

Lingering over her morning coffee, Anastasia kept her eyes trained on the entrance to the dining room. Finally she decided that it was stupid to wait any longer. The actress might not even be coming down to breakfast.

Getting up from the table, she pondered the situation. If there was any chance to get what she needed to show that Kyle Quigley was a predator, the actress was it. Anastasia had to persuade her to go in with the hidden camera while she had a sleep treatment.

That was a lot to ask. But she would make an emotional, moral, and professional appeal to the actress. This guy had to be stopped. The actress would be using her professional skills to catch him. And, as a bonus, she might even get some publicity out of it.

Anastasia walked into the lobby, went to one of the house phones, and asked to be connected to the actress's room.

"We have no one registered under that name," said the operator.

Of course, thought Anastasia as she hung up. The actress hadn't registered under her own name.

Anastasia was undeterred. She *had* to find her.

CHAPTER

76

PIPER RODE TO THE CALLBACK audition full of excitement and anticipation. She returned to Elysium crestfallen. The callback was a disaster.

She'd been stiff with nerves. She repeatedly flubbed the copy they gave her to read and failed miserably in the improvisation she was asked to perform with the male actors who'd also been chosen to return. As she walked out, her face was flushed with embarrassment.

What was the matter with her? How could she do so well one day and then be such a mess the next? Why couldn't she just relax and remember that most of this was out of her control? How could she be so prepared yet feel so uncomfortable? All she had to do was be herself and show that she was capable. That was easy, wasn't it?

As all these questions churned in her head, she felt the familiar survival instinct kick in. *That happened. It's over. Just keep going.*

So, with tears in her eyes, Piper slipped into the Town Car and headed back to the spa.

WHEN SHE REACHED THE SAFETY of her suite, she flopped down on the bed, feeling discouraged and frustrated. Then she thought of Wendy and Esperanza. Piper realized she should be incredibly grateful that her problems were so relatively small.

She knew it was ridiculous to let herself get so down. So she hadn't nailed the callback. There would be others. At least now she wouldn't have to worry about having to balance the commercial shoot with making the wedding cake.

She lay on her back for a while, looking up at the ceiling. This wasn't going to make her feel any better, lying around and wallowing in self-pity. She should get up, put on her bathing suit, and go down to the pool. Swimming some laps—*that* would make her feel better. Then she could finish the final cake sketch and take it over to Jillian later for approval.

THE ACTRESS WAS AT THE pool. Piper spotted her right away, and she considered going over and sitting next to her.

Piper grabbed a towel from the cabana and walked toward the actress. The actress smiled at her. Piper was emboldened.

"Is this chair taken?" she asked.

"No, go right ahead," said the actress. "I could use some company."

Piper draped the towel on the lounge chair, took the sunscreen from her bag, and slathered herself with it. Adjusting her straw hat, she stretched out and heaved a long sigh.

"Rough day?" said the actress.

"I just came from a terrible callback," said Piper.

"You're an actress?"

"Yes," said Piper. "I'm trying to be."

"It's a tough business. Brutal sometimes," said the actress. "It took me years of suffering rejection after rejection, and then I got a supporting role in a sitcom, which led to a spinoff of my character in a show of her own. Before I knew it, I was being offered movie parts."

Piper nodded. "I loved that show," she said. "I watched it pretty much all through middle school."

"Ouch," said the actress. "I suddenly feel so old. Although I shouldn't say 'suddenly.'"

"Please, you're not old," Piper protested.

"Thanks, kiddo. But let's face it, I'm in the 'character actor' years. And I'm not ever going to get the kind of parts

I used to, no matter what magic they work on me here to make me look younger."

Piper wasn't sure what to say. The actress was speaking the truth.

"Here's what I try to remember," the actress continued. "Everything's bad until it's good. If this is what you really want, then you just have to hang in there until you get to the good times."

Piper considered her words. "I guess I really have no other choice," she said. "Acting is what I've wanted since I was a little kid. I can't even imagine giving it up."

"You have your answer, then," said the actress. "Just keep at it, day by day. Follow all your leads, continue your acting classes, go for every audition you can. Suddenly it will reach critical mass and you'll catch a lucky break."

Piper brightened. "Thanks for that," she said. "I needed it."

"You're welcome," said the actress. She dug into her bag and pulled out a pad and pen. "Here's my e-mail address. Feel free to stay in touch and let me know how you're progressing."

As Piper took the piece of paper, the actress looked at her watch. "I've got to get going."

"Well, again, thanks so much," said Piper, smiling up at her. "I really appreciate it."

CHAPTER

77

THE ACTRESS WALKED TO THE skin-care center, reminding herself why she was going to do this. The reporter had been persuasive. Anastasia's point, that a pervert had to be stopped, hit home. Appealing to the actress's sense of right and wrong had worked. Anastasia's flattery about her acting skills hadn't hurt either. Nor had the reminder about the publicity this could engender.

At first the actress had been stunned. The idea that an Elysium employee could be perpetrating such heinous acts was mind-blowing. Even more, she'd felt the hair on the back of her neck rise when Anastasia reminded her of the unexplained bruise on her thigh.

Had that creep actually done something to her while she slept?

Any trepidation the actress had been feeling was replaced by anger. Outrage was a strong emotion, and strong emotion had fueled some of her best work. She was about to turn in another great performance.

She could imagine the headlines now.

ACTRESS BRINGS DOWN HOUSE OF HORRORS!

Publicity like that would put her back on the radar screens of producers and studio heads. Publicity like that would get her working again.

CHAPTER

78

KYLE SMILED BROADLY AND INSINCERELY as he welcomed the actress into his treatment room.

Why is she insisting on another sleep treatment so soon? She just had one!

He liked to think that on some unconscious level she had enjoyed what he'd done for her and wanted more. But he had to stay alert for anything suspicious. Piper Donovan's visit the day before had left him wary.

He watched as the actress came in and put her bag down on the counter. Did she always do that? Didn't she usually come in without her bag, having stashed it in one of the dressing-room lockers? He couldn't remember, but he did recall that Piper had put her bag down in the same place yesterday.

First he wiped the injection spot with numbing lidocaine.

"As you already know, this won't hurt a bit," said Kyle as he inserted the fine-gauge needle in the actress's arm. "Just relax and begin to count."

The actress took a deep breath and slowly exhaled. "One, two, three . . ."

Her eyes closed at six. By twelve she had stopped counting.

Kyle studied her, reaching out to gently turn her face from side to side. The surgery Vernon had performed was expertly done. The scars next to her ears were barely visible, and her skin hadn't been pulled too tight. Though the hands of time couldn't be rolled back completely, she was still very attractive.

He felt himself getting excited. Then, as he began to lift her smock, he remembered. Kyle walked over to the counter, opened the actress's bag, and rummaged through. He found the camera.

The hag was trying to catch him!

Kyle felt his face grow hot. His heart pounded as he considered the terrifyingly close call and its implications. Was the actress working with Piper Donovan and that Anastasia Wilcox, the one with the short, dark hair? Were they conspiring to expose what he'd been doing?

He turned to look at the actress, lying asleep and vulnerable. His first instinct was to go over and wring her neck. Instantly, he decided that wouldn't work. Even if he killed her, there would be no way to get rid of her body without being seen.

Another option was injecting her vein with air. That would cause a fatal heart attack that could look as if it were natural. But then he would have to explain what she was doing in the treatment room in the first place. And though an autopsy wouldn't detect what had caused her death, it would show the drug that had put the actress to sleep.

Kyle went to the sink and splashed cold water on his face. He tried to calm himself. He had to think rationally.

Settle down. Get ahold of yourself.

What did the actress really have on him anyway?

He took the camera out of the bag and hit REWIND. Then he watched the images play back. Pictures of the actress walking over and climbing up onto the massage table. Pictures of him injecting her. Pictures of her counting and falling into unconsciousness. Pictures of him standing over the actress and turning her face from side to side. Pictures of him walking toward the camera, followed by blackness as he blocked the camera's view.

Kyle erased the video, turned the camera off, and returned it to the bag. Then he continued with the sleep treatment.

CHAPTER

79

B EN PULLED ON HIS SPORT jacket and gave Jillian a kiss. "You're sure it's all right with you?" he asked.

"Of course it is," she said. "You don't have to ask my permission to go out with a friend."

"I know," said Ben, "but I hate to leave you right now."

"I'll be fine," said Jillian. "I love you madly, Ben, but I can survive without you for a few hours. Go, have dinner with Paul. You haven't seen him since you did your residencies together."

Ben shook his head. "I didn't think he'd actually come when I invited him out for the wedding. Now he's out here for the week by himself. The least I can do is buy him a few drinks and some dinner."

"Where are you taking him?" asked Jillian as she reached out and smoothed Ben's lapel.

"I made a reservation at the Chateau Marmont," said Ben. "I thought he'd enjoy a few celebrity sightings."

"Well, that's the place for it," said Jillian. "I love going there."

"You sure you don't want to join us?" asked Ben.

"No," she answered. "You guys should enjoy catching up all by yourselves. You don't need me tagging along. Besides, Piper is coming over tonight to show me her sketches for the wedding cake."

CHAPTER

80

I DON'T UNDERSTAND," SAID THE ACTRESS when Anastasia came to her room. "There's nothing here."

"Let me look," said Anastasia, taking the camera from her. She fiddled with the buttons and squinted at the small screen. Nothing.

"I don't understand," said the actress. "I know I turned it on. Why didn't it record?"

"Was it still on when you took it out of your bag?" asked Anastasia.

The actress looked uncomfortable. "No, it wasn't, but I thought the camera had just run out of record time and turned itself off."

"Well, even if that was the case, the video you recorded would still be there."

The two women stared at each other.

"You don't think Kyle went through my bag, found the camera, and turned it off, do you?" asked the actress.

"That's exactly what I think," Anastasia answered. "And I think he erased any video that was on there as well."

CHAPTER

81

I T WAS EIGHT O'CLOCK WHEN Jillian welcomed Piper into the cottage. A thin, gray-haired man was sitting on the sofa in the living room. In front of him, papers were spread out on the coffee table.

"Piper, this is Hudson Sherwood," said Jillian. "Hudson has just returned to Elysium as our assistant director."

"Nice to meet you," said Piper, trying to recall where she'd heard that name.

"Piper has come all the way from New Jersey to make our wedding cake," said Jillian.

"Is that so?" asked Hudson. "You must be exceptionally talented."

"She is," said Jillian. "You'll see on Saturday, Hudson."

"I'm looking forward to it." He smiled at Piper, a smile that she somehow sensed was insincere.

Hudson looked down at the papers on the table and ran his hands through his receding hair. "I think we've covered everything, then, Jillian." He began to gather up the papers.

"Thanks so much for coming over and for staying so late," said Jillian. "It's great of you to take over the scheduling already."

Hudson stood. "Not a problem," he answered. "I hope you take advantage of having me here to help you as much as possible, Jillian. I want to take everything I can off your hands."

As Piper watched him walk to the door, she remembered the article she'd read online. Hudson Sherwood had been the director of Elysium until he was replaced by Jillian Abernathy. That must have been very hard to swallow.

Now he was back, taking orders from her.

"Oh, Piper, I love it!" exclaimed Jillian as she looked at the sketches of the wedding cake. "It's absolutely beautiful."

Piper smiled with pleasure. "I'm so glad you like it."

"Will the smallest layer really look like our gazebo here at Elysium?" Jillian asked, pointing to the rendering.

"Mm-hmm. I can make the railings with gum paste and the curlicues with icing. And each of the angels on top of the cake will be as close a replica to the angel on the top of the real gazebo as I can make."

"It's absolutely perfect," said Jillian, leaning over and giving Piper a hug. "It's the first thing that's gone right with this wedding. Thank you so much."

"You're welcome," said Piper, silently praying that she could execute her paper-and-pencil design just as well on the actual wedding cake.

"Let's have a glass of wine to celebrate," said Jillian.

Looking at the smile on Jillian's face, Piper didn't have the heart to turn her down.

CHAPTER

82

GEORGE DROPPED HIS ROBE ONTO a chair. He shivered in the nippy night air as he rushed over to the hot tub. Not stopping to test the water, he stepped in, lowering his bulky body and immersing himself.

He was only taking Vernon up on his offer to help himself to all the amenities offered at Elysium. He needed to relax, and he knew it. The flask of whiskey he'd brought with him would provide assistance.

The knot in his chest was ever present, and he hadn't been able to eat much since getting the news that Wendy couldn't be helped. He probably should have asked Dr. Ben to put him on some antianxiety medication or at least a couple of tranquilizers to help get him through this wrenching time.

"But I've got you, don't I? My old buddy Jim Beam will

get me through," said George as he twisted the cap off the flask. He took a long swallow, then another.

George was glad that nobody else was around and he had the hot tub all to himself. He didn't want anyone to see him. A grown man crying was not a pretty sight.

The punch of the whiskey and the heat of the bubbling water warmed him, inside and out. He felt the beads of perspiration gathering on his brow. He took another couple of swigs.

Leaning his head on the edge of the hot tub and looking up at the stars, George wished he could find some peace. But he didn't see how that was possible. His daughter's life had been ruined. How could he come to terms with that?

He finished off the contents of the flask. Again, he couldn't get over the unfairness of it all. Whatever happened in Wendy's life, it was improbable—no, impossible—that she would have a life like the one Vernon Abernathy's daughter would live. Did Jillian know the havoc her father had caused? Did it even occur to her how Wendy was suffering?

Slowly George stood up. He wobbled, and his foot slipped off one of the steps as he tried to climb out of the hot tub. He fell back into the water.

As he righted himself and lumbered out, George didn't even feel the cold night air. He struggled to find the arms of his robe. Finally he managed to get it on and headed in the direction of Jillian's cottage.

CHAPTER

83

"OH, I'D BETTER GET GOING. It's after nine," said Piper as she looked at her watch. She finished the glass of wine and gathered up her cake sketches. She was about to leave when there was a knock on the cottage door.

"I wonder who that is," said Jillian. "I'm not expecting anyone."

When Jillian opened the door, Piper could see a heavyset man wearing a terry-cloth bathrobe. His hair was wet, and his face was flushed. He swayed as Jillian greeted him.

"Hello, Mr. Ellis. Is everything all right?"

"No, everything is *not* all right," he said loudly. "As a matter of fact, nothing is all right. Nothing at all." He leaned forward and looked into the room, spotting Piper.

"Ah, what do we have here?" he asked. "Another pretty

girl. Isn't that nice? Two pretty girls enjoying their lives while mine sits all alone, hiding in shame."

Piper felt sorry for the man, who she now realized was Wendy's father. He was clearly drunk and upset, as she supposed he had every right to be. But Piper also felt apprehensive. There was anger and desperation in his deep voice.

She extended her hand. "I'm Piper Donovan, Mr. Ellis. I know Wendy."

George's facial expression softened a bit. "Oh, Piper, yes. You've been so kind to my Wendy. Thank you for that."

"There's no reason to thank me," said Piper. "I enjoyed having dinner with her. I hope we can spend some more time together before I leave."

"I hope so, too," said George. He turned to face Jillian. "Wendy's been here for a long time. I'm wondering how many attempts *you've* made to reach out to her."

Jillian looked uncomfortable. "I wanted to visit Wendy, but my father and Ben didn't think it was such a good idea."

"Oh? And why's that?" asked George.

Jillian was silent.

George raised his voice again as he repeated the question. "Why didn't you go to see Wendy?"

"Please, Mr. Ellis," pleaded Jillian. "Why don't I call my father and ask him to come over here?"

"Don't bother," sneered George. "The last thing I need is Vernon Abernathy spouting his crap. But I'll tell you something. Your father and that handsome fiancé of yours didn't want you to go see Wendy because they thought it would depress her. Or at least that's the reason they probably gave you. The real reason is something entirely different."

George grabbed the doorjamb to steady himself. "The reason they wanted to keep you away from Wendy is that they didn't want to upset *me*. They weren't worried about depressing Wendy—they were worried about *me*, looking at your face and comparing it to Wendy's. They didn't want to make *me* any madder than they knew I already was. They were worried I'd sue and bring this place down."

As George turned away, he continued to mutter, slurring his words. "Somebody's got to pay for what happened to my Wendy. Somebody's got to pay."

CHAPTER

84

TONIGHT IS THE NIGHT. THERE'S *no point in waiting any longer.*

Everything is ready. The cooler was transferred to the rear of the golf cart. The turpentine-soaked rags were inserted in the bottle necks to serve as wicks to the flammable liquid inside.

Once the Molotov cocktails are hurled into the window of Jillian's cottage, the golf cart will provide me with a speedy escape, disappearing silently into the night.

CHAPTER

85

THE PHONE WAS RINGING. It was rare that anyone called, especially at night.

Sister Mary Noelle was saying her prayers in her room. She rose from her knees, went out into the hall, and picked up the receiver.

"Monastery of the Angels. May I help you?" she answered softly.

"Nina?"

Sister Mary Noelle recognized her sister's voice and sensed that something was wrong. "Jillian. Is everything all right?"

"No, Nina, everything is terrible."

Between whimpers Jillian told Sister Mary Noelle about George Ellis's visit. "I'm scared of what he might do!" she cried. "I'm all by myself now."

"Where's Ben?" asked Sister Mary Noelle.

"He's out with a friend," said Jillian. "Or at least that's where he's supposed to be. His cell phone goes immediately into voice mail, and I called the Chateau Marmont, where he said he was having dinner, and they say he's not there."

"Did you call Dad?" Sister Mary Noelle asked.

"No, he has so much on his plate already. I don't want to give him any more to worry about." Jillian pleaded, "I want to be with you, Nina. Can I come over?"

"Oh, Jillian. I'm so sorry, but that won't work." Sister Mary Noelle lowered her voice to a whisper. "I can't ask Mother Mary Dominic to have a night visitor."

"Maybe she'd make an exception, since I'm your sister."

"No, Jillian. That's not going to happen."

"Well, can you get out and come over here?" Jillian asked hopefully.

Sister Mary Noelle thought about the car in the parking lot. She had the keys. She could probably sneak out and drive over to Elysium without anyone in the convent even knowing. That would be deceitful. But Jillian was her sister, and Jillian needed her.

"Let me see what I can do," said Sister Mary Noelle.

CHAPTER

86

S HE COULDN'T SLEEP. SHE WASN'T the least bit tired.
The actress watched television for a while, flipping through the channels. After the eleven o'clock news, she turned off the set. Picking up a magazine, she began flipping through the pages. The pictures of the young, nubile models in the advertisements depressed her. She tossed the magazine onto the floor beside the bed.

She got up and walked out onto the terrace, pulling her robe closer to warm herself. Though cool, it was a beautiful, clear night. The moon was almost full, its beams illuminating Elysium's grounds.

Her thoughts turned to Kyle Quigley and his sleep treatments. She was disappointed she hadn't accomplished the goal of capturing his alleged misconduct. Maybe there wasn't even anything to catch. Maybe the reporter had it all wrong.

The actress raised her hand to feel her face. The skin was soft and smooth. At least the time in Kyle's treatment room hadn't been a total loss.

She went back inside, knowing that she was not going to be able to fall asleep yet. Maybe a walk would do her good. A stroll in the night air might relax her. The actress went to the bureau and took out a heavy sweatshirt. Pulling off her nightgown, she noticed a fresh black-and-blue mark.

As she walked through the lobby, the actress waved to the clerk at the registration desk.

"I'm going for a little walk," she called. "If I'm not back in half an hour, send the cavalry."

As she went out the door, the actress felt confident. Elysium was a safe haven, carefully guarded so no undesirables could get in. She also had her cell phone with her.

She started down the lit path, passing the art studio and the apothecary. She stepped up her pace as she approached the yoga, spinning, and Pilates house. Just before she got to the end of the walkway, the actress stopped short.

She pulled out her cell phone and dialed 911.

CHAPTER

87

THE HEAVY FLASHLIGHT BRIGHTENS THE *way to Jillian's cottage. The golf cart pulls up slowly and silently comes to a stop. Everything else is done very quickly. Opening the chest, taking out the bottles, lighting the wicks, and throwing them. Propelled through the air from close range, the firebombs hit their marks.*

The window glass shatters. Red and orange flames explode as the bottles hit the floor inside the cottage. The fire begins to spread in a fierce, destructive blaze.

The flames are mesmerizing as they dance. It's tempting to stay and watch, but there's no time to waste.

A glance in the direction of the path coming down from the main building reveals a woman standing beneath the light.

The golf cart rides away into the darkness. When it's in a hidden place, it comes to a stop. The sounds of distant sirens cut through the night air.

Are the police already on their way to Elysium? Has the woman called for help?

Think. Think.

This isn't the way it was supposed to go. No one was supposed to see anything. What was that woman doing out in the middle of the night? What exactly did she actually see?

Maybe she won't be able to identify me. She was illuminated by the light on the path, but I wasn't. Do I dare let it go and hope for the best?

But if she did see me, I have to kill her before the police come. I have to kill her before she tells anyone who she saw.

The sirens are getting closer.

CHAPTER

88

THE ACTRESS SPRINTED TOWARD THE cottage. She tried to open the front door, but it was locked. She ran around to the back. It was locked, too.

She pounded on the door. "Fire! Fire!" she yelled. "Wake up, wake up! Fire!"

She coughed repeatedly as thick black smoke entered her lungs. Ferocious flames poured from the broken window. She couldn't tell if it was a bedroom window. If it was, the person sleeping inside could already be dead.

The actress could hear the sirens in the distance. Would they get there in time? Was it already too late?

As her heart hammered and these thoughts raced through her mind, she didn't hear the golf cart pull up behind her.

CHAPTER

89

THE BLARE OF THE SIRENS woke Piper. She got out of bed and hurried over to the balcony. She watched as fire trucks and police cars sped into the courtyard, their flashing red and blue lights cutting through the darkness.

She pulled on a pair of jeans, slipped her feet into sandals, and ran out the door. When she got downstairs, the lobby was full of other alarmed guests trying to learn what was happening. One woman was crying hysterically. Piper made her way through the crowd and went outside.

She followed in the direction that the rescue workers were going. It was the path she'd taken just hours before when she went to Jillian's cottage. Her pulse raced as she saw flames in the distance.

"Oh, my God. It *is* Jillian's," Piper whispered to herself

as the cottage came into view. Police spotlights had been set up to illuminate the front of the bungalow. Firefighters were breaking all the windows and training their hoses on the openings to spray water inside the house.

More guests and Elysium staff members hurried down the hill to watch. Piper searched their faces, looking for Jillian. She couldn't find her.

WHEN THE FIRE WAS FINALLY extinguished, the acrid stench of smoke filled the air. While the scorched cottage remained standing, most of its exterior was covered with heavy black soot.

"Chief, you gotta take a look at this!" called a fireman.

Piper broke off from the crowd and followed unobtrusively, making her way across the soggy grass to the rear yard of the cottage. Several firefighters and police officers were gathered in a circle, looking down at the ground. Piper watched with increasing dread as one of the policemen broke off from the group, bent over, and vomited. The space left open by his departure afforded her a better view.

The body of a blond woman was lying facedown in the dirt.

Piper saw Vernon Abernathy pushing through the crowd. He rushed right past her to get to the spot where the cops and firemen were gathered.

"Jillian! Oh, my God, is that Jillian?" Vernon yelled.

Irene Abernathy reached out to pull her husband back. "Don't, Vernon! Don't look!" she screamed.

Ignoring his wife, Vernon pushed aside one of the officers. He knelt on the ground beside the woman. The back of her head was smashed in, revealing mangled brain matter. Her blond hair was matted, thick with blood.

Somebody produced a flashlight and trained the beam on the lifeless body. Vernon leaned in closer as the body was turned over. Everyone was quiet while they waited for him to identify his daughter.

Slowly Vernon stood up. "That's not Jillian," he said in a low voice. "That's not my daughter."

Piper heard his pronouncement. Her first reaction was one of relief. Her next emotion was confusion.

If it wasn't Jillian, then who was it? And where *was* Jillian? Was she still inside the ravaged cottage?

Firefighters were searching the cottage, looking for any survivors or victims. It seemed like an eternity before one came out and yelled, "All clear! There's nobody in here!"

Piper witnessed Irene crying as she and Vernon clung together.

"Dear God, where is Jillian?" he pleaded.

And just then a woman's voice called out, "Here I am."

JILLIAN AND BEN STOOD THERE as they were swarmed by the people who had feared that she'd been killed. Piper listened as she explained.

"I'm so sorry. I needed to get out, and I just went for a ride," she said. "While I was driving, Ben called and asked me to meet him and his friend. They'd decided not to go to the Chateau. They were at STK, the steak house on La Cienega."

"Thank the dear Lord you're all right," said Vernon, pulling Jillian to him and hugging her.

"I'm sorry that I scared you, Daddy," she said.

"Yeah," said Ben. "I'm sorry that *all* of you went through this." He put his arm around Irene, whose face was drained of color.

Piper glanced over to the spot where the dead woman's body lay. She noticed Anastasia standing nearby as the body was lifted onto a stretcher. The journalist was holding up her cell phone. Piper realized that Anastasia was recording video of the scene.

She broke off from the group, walked over to Anastasia, and tapped her on the arm. Anastasia turned, saw Piper, and then turned back to the cell-phone camera.

"This is unbelievable, isn't it?" said Anastasia.

"Awful," said Piper. "Did you get close enough to see the woman's face? Do you know who it is?"

"Hold on a minute," said Anastasia. She twisted at the waist as her camera followed the stretcher being carried away. When the stretcher had been loaded into the ambulance and the truck had driven off, Anastasia stopped recording. She texted something and pushed another few buttons before closing the cell phone and turning to Piper.

"It's our friend, the actress," she whispered.

Piper stared at Anastasia, not fully comprehending what she was saying.

"The dead woman is the *actress,*" said Anastasia. "I talked her into taking another sleep treatment today and bringing the camera with her. She didn't get the goods on Kyle, but we suspected that he's onto us. Now I'm thinking that's why she's dead."

Before she could utter a word, Piper saw something moving into her field of vision. It was Vernon Abernathy, charging at Anastasia. He grabbed her by the arm.

"Give it to me," he sneered.

"What are you talking about?" asked Anastasia, trying to wiggle free.

"Give me your damned phone!" demanded Vernon. "I *thought* you were the one who took the video when Esperanza was killed. Now I *know* it was you. I'm not going to have you splashing tonight's ugliness around the world."

"Too late," Anastasia said with a weak smile. "The video has already been sent."

PIPER'S HAND SHOOK AS SHE inserted the key card into the lock. She shed her clothes, depositing them in one of the plastic laundry bags in the closet. She held her forearm up to her nose. Her body smelled of smoke.

She went into the bathroom and looked at herself in the mirror. Her face was covered with soot and ash. Her long blond hair was tangled.

Piper got into the shower and turned the water on, as hot as she could stand. She let the rushing water and soft soap wash away the smell and grime. She could see the water turn black at her feet before it drained.

If only she could wash away the thoughts that were going through her mind.

The actress was dead. What had Lillie Ulster been doing at Jillian's cottage in the first place? If she hadn't been killed in the fire, someone had killed her. Who and why?

Piper wished she'd had more time to talk to Anastasia, but Vernon had ordered his security team to immediately escort the reporter off the property. Piper was still trying to assimilate the information that Anastasia had gotten the actress to help her with her investigation. Was that the reason the actress had been murdered? Besides being a pervert, was Kyle Quigley a killer? Finally, was the murder of the actress connected in some way to the murder of Esperanza Flores and the acid attack all those months ago?

Turning off the shower, Piper squeezed the water from her hair and twisted a towel around it. She dried herself with a luxurious bath sheet, enjoying the soothing sensation against her skin. Taking a spa bathrobe from the hook on the wall, Piper wrapped herself in it and padded on bare feet to the bedroom.

She ached to talk to Jack.

Suddenly it didn't matter one bit who called whom first.

CHAPTER

90

WHAT THE . . . ?"
Jack looked at the bedside clock as he reached for
the phone. Who was calling at four-thirty in the morning? A
call at this hour was usually not good news.

He inhaled deeply when he saw the number displayed on
the caller ID panel.

Piper!

As he picked up the phone, he wondered how this conversation would go. Jack decided that it would be a good idea
to try to play it cool.

"Hello?"

"Hi, Jack. It's me."

"Hi, me."

"Sorry for waking you."

"That's okay. How's it going out there?"

"It's not so great, Jack."

"What's wrong?" He sat up and turned on the lamp. He listened as Piper told him about the fire, the murder of the actress, Anastasia's investigation of Kyle Quigley, and the part Piper herself had played in it.

"What are you, crazy?" asked Jack, raising his voice. "What are you *doing*?"

"I just wanted to help. He didn't put me to sleep, Jack. Nothing bad happened."

"What do you call the murder of Lillie Ulster?" asked Jack. "Did you ever think that could have been you?"

Piper was quiet.

"You've got to go to the police, Piper, and tell them what your reporter friend was working on and that Lillie Ulster had gotten involved in helping her, too. Hang up the phone and call the cops right away."

Jack's heart raced as he put down the receiver. The thought that Piper was involved in something like this terrified him. Despite her father's best efforts to prepare her, she was too altruistic and trusting. She didn't grasp that she was in danger.

He got out of bed and walked over to his desk. He sat down, turned on the computer, and began checking flight schedules.

So much for playing it cool.

CHAPTER

91

JACK WAS RIGHT. SHE HAD to go to the police. But she should tell the Abernathys first. They had paid for her to come out to Elysium; she was working for them. It was the right thing to alert them about what could be happening at their spa.

Piper thought about Anastasia. It was a betrayal of sorts to reveal the story the reporter had been investigating. But the fire and the murder of the actress had changed things. The stakes were much higher now.

The adrenaline that had been pumping through her system had abated. The shower had been soothing, and the conversation with Jack, even though he'd been adamant that she go to the police, had been comforting. It was such a relief to talk to him again.

Suddenly Piper felt very, very tired.

She fell asleep, resolved that she would go to both the Abernathys and the police in the morning.

CHAPTER

92

As DAWN BROKE, NEWS VANS with satellite dishes and throngs of reporters and camera crews were gathered outside the gates of Elysium. Hudson drove up, slowing and rolling down the car window. Microphones were instantly thrust through.

"Who are you?" asked a reporter.

"My name is Hudson Sherwood."

"Are you a guest, or do you work here?"

"I'm the assistant director of Elysium." Having to identify himself with the diminished title irked him.

"What do you know about Lillie Ulster's murder?"

"Not a thing," said Hudson. "I'm just getting here."

"Will someone from Elysium come out and give us a statement?"

"I would imagine so," said Hudson. "But I think it's fair to say that everyone at Elysium is devastated. We will be giving the police our full cooperation."

As Hudson drove away, he made an effort to keep the smile off his face.

CHAPTER

93

JILLIAN HADN'T SLEPT ALL NIGHT. She lay in the bed in her father's house, the coverlet pulled up to her chin as she worried.

If she'd been asleep in her cottage last night, she would have been killed. It was clear that someone was out to get her. Esperanza had been maimed and murdered because of that. Now Lillie Ulster was dead, too.

As the morning light trickled through the crack beneath the window shade, Jillian made her decision.

Nobody should get married under such a black cloud. She was going to call off the wedding.

CHAPTER

94

A POLICE CAR AND A DARK gray sedan were parked in the driveway. As she walked up to the house, Piper reasoned it was probably for the best. She'd be able to tell the Abernathys and the police at the same time.

Irene Abernathy opened the door. Her face was without makeup, and her skin looked pale. She didn't appear happy to see Piper.

"Oh, dear, this isn't the best time," said Irene, self-consciously smoothing her messy hair.

"I know," said Piper. "And I hate to bother all of you right now, but there's something I have to tell you."

"Well, the police detectives are here," said Irene. "It will have to wait until later."

"No," said Piper. "They need to hear it, too."

Irene looked uncertain but opened the door wide for Piper to enter.

VERNON, JILLIAN, AND BEN WERE at the dining-room table. Two men in suits sat across from them. One was taking notes. Through the window Piper could see a uniformed officer standing outside on the patio.

She stood in the doorway, listening and waiting for her chance to speak.

"Well, as far as the fire is concerned, our investigators know it was arson. It appears somebody tossed a couple of Molotov cocktails through the window." The detective looked at Jillian. "Is there anyone you can think of who would want to hurt you, Miss Abernathy?"

Jillian closed her eyes and shook her head. "This isn't the first time I've been through this," she said. "I couldn't think of anyone when Esperanza was attacked with acid or when she was murdered. I can't think of anyone now."

"What about you, Dr. Abernathy? Do you have any enemies? Any unhappy guests, patients, or employees?" The detective consulted his notes. "At the time of the acid attack, you mentioned a disgruntled employee that you'd fired."

Vernon nodded. "Hudson Sherwood, but he's working at Elysium again. I don't think he's a threat."

"You never know," said the detective. "He could still be holding a grudge."

"Daddy," said Jillian, reaching out and touching her father's arm, "with everything that's happened, I forgot to tell you that George Ellis came to my cottage last night. He'd been drinking. The poor man is very bitter."

The detectives exchanged glances. "Who is George Ellis?" one asked.

"He's the father of one of our patients," said Vernon.

Irene walked behind her husband and put her hands on his shoulders. "His daughter's surgery didn't go well. Vernon just had to let her know over the weekend that there isn't anything he can do to repair the damage."

"Well, we have a couple of good leads. Let's see where they take us." The detective closed his notebook. "We're thinking the same person who started the fire killed Lillie Ulster. Whoever it was is pretty damn vicious. Whatever was used to bash in her skull sure did the job. Brutally."

As the detectives stood up, Piper stepped forward. "Wait," she said. "There's something else you should know about."

She explained what Anastasia had suspected about Kyle Quigley's sleep treatments. "When he wouldn't give her a treatment, Anastasia asked me to try," Piper finished. "I went to Kyle with a hidden camera to record him, but he said I wasn't a candidate. After that, Anastasia asked Lillie Ulster to do the same thing. She'd had the treatment before, and afterward she had a really ugly bruise but couldn't remember where she'd gotten it."

"Did Miss Ulster get anywhere with the secret camera?" asked one of the detectives.

"I don't think so," said Piper. "But before Anastasia left Elysium, she told me that she thought Kyle had something to do with Lillie's death."

The detectives turned to Vernon. "We'll need your permission to search the premises. In particular, Kyle Quigley's treatment room."

Vernon looked stunned. "Of course," he said quietly.

"Good," said the detective. "And we'll get a search warrant for Quigley's home."

PIPER BEGAN TO FOLLOW AS Vernon and Ben escorted the detectives out of the kitchen.

"Wait," said Jillian. "I need to talk to you, Piper. Can you stay for a few minutes?"

"Sure," said Piper, pulling out a chair and sitting down.

"How about a cup of tea?" asked Irene.

"That would be great. Thank you," said Piper. She turned and looked expectantly at Jillian.

"There's not going to be a wedding, Piper," she said. "With all that's going on, this just isn't the time."

"Oh, Jillian," said Piper. "I am so, so sorry. But I totally get it. I really do."

Irene put a teacup in front of Piper. "So you won't need to make the wedding cake," she said.

"Of course not," said Piper.

"You're still welcome to stay here at Elysium for as long as you want," said Jillian. "But I can't imagine you'd enjoy being here now, with this nightmare going on."

PIPER FELT DEFLATED AND VERY sad as she walked back to the main building. So much pointless destruction. Esperanza Flores and Lillie Ulster were dead, while Jillian and Ben's wedding plans had been blown to bits.

How was it all connected? That was for the police to figure out now. Jillian was right: There was no reason for Piper to stay at Elysium any longer.

As she got to the courtyard, her plan was to go inside and check the flights back to Newark. But while she was walking through the lobby, her phone rang. It was Gabe.

"They loved you, doll. You got the part!"

Piper stopped in her tracks. "You're kidding me. I don't believe it."

"Believe it, babe. They're shooting the commercial on Friday morning."

Piper cocked her head, not comprehending. "But I did such a bad job at the callback."

"You simply don't know your own talent, Piper," said

Gabe. "They said you were delightful, and I have absolutely no doubt you were."

When the phone call ended, Piper remembered what Lillie Ulster had said when she'd given her the pep talk just yesterday at the pool.

Everything's bad until it's good.

CHAPTER

95

JILLIAN WROTE THE E-MAIL HERSELF.

DEAR FRIENDS AND FAMILY,

FORGIVE US FOR SENDING YOU NEWS LIKE THIS IN SUCH
A SEEMINGLY IMPERSONAL WAY. FOR REASONS THAT YOU
CAN EASILY SEE ON TELEVISION OR READ ABOUT IN THE
NEWSPAPER, HAVING A WEDDING NOW JUST DOESN'T FEEL
RIGHT.

WE ARE HEARTBROKEN ABOUT CANCELING OUR MARRIAGE
CEREMONY ON SATURDAY. WE APOLOGIZE TO ANY AND ALL OF
YOU WHO HAVE BEEN INCONVENIENCED, BUT WE KNOW THAT
YOU WILL UNDERSTAND WHY WE ARE DOING THIS.

WE ASK YOU TO KEEP ESPERANZA FLORES, LILLIE ULSTER,

AND THEIR FAMILIES IN YOUR PRAYERS.

LOVE,

JILLIAN AND BEN

She read the message over and hit the SEND button.

CHAPTER

96

Mother Mary Dominic called Sister Mary Noelle to her office.

"Yes, Mother?"

"Sit down, Sister." Mother Superior looked grim.

As she lowered herself into the chair opposite Mother's desk, Sister Mary Noelle saw the newspaper lying on the desk.

"What is it, Mother? Is something wrong?"

"I'm afraid there is, Sister." The older nun passed her the newspaper.

Sister Noelle gasped at the headline.

ACTRESS DEAD AS FIRE BURNS ELITE SPA.

THERE WERE TEARS IN SISTER Mary Noelle's eyes after she finished reading the account of what had happened the night before at Elysium. Immediately, she asked herself if things would have been different if she'd gone to visit Jillian as she let her sister think she might. After Jillian's phone call, Sister Mary Noelle had thought about it and decided not to go. It was one thing to go out into the world to do the external work of the convent, but it was quite another to sneak out without Mother's permission.

"I'm sorry, Sister," said Mother Prioress.

"Thank you, Mother. May I ask your permission to go to Elysium? I want to be there for my sister and father."

Mother Superior shook her head, and Sister Mary Noelle closed her eyes as she felt immediate disappointment.

"What you may do," said Mother Mary Dominic, "is ask your family to come see you here. Then you can all pray for God's mercy together."

CHAPTER

97

Aᴠᴛᴇʀ Vᴇʀɴᴏɴ ᴀɴᴅ Bᴇɴ ʟᴇғᴛ to go to their offices in the main building, Jillian and Irene sipped tea in the den. Irene repeatedly clicked the remote control, surfing channels to catch noon news accounts. The Elysium story was getting major play.

"Turn it off, will you, Irene?" asked Jillian. "I can't look at it anymore."

Just as the television screen went to black, the phone rang. A few moments later, the housekeeper came in to say that Sister Mary Noelle was on the line.

"Oh, Nina!" cried Jillian. "It's so horrible!"

Irene could hear only Jillian's side of the conversation.

"Yes, I'm all right. . . . Daddy's so upset. I'm really worried about him. Elysium is his life. . . . No, no, don't worry about not getting here last night, Nina. After a while I figured you weren't able to get out. And that's probably what *saved* my life. I went for a drive to clear my head, and then I met Ben and his friend, so I wasn't there when the cottage was set on fire."

Jillian was quiet for a few moments, listening and nodding. She finally said, "Yes, that's a good idea. I'd like that. But I don't think Daddy will come. He's up to his neck, dealing with the police, the insurance companies, and the media." After a few more moments, Jillian said, "Oh, no! I completely forgot about it. Poor guy. What a miserable way to spend your birthday."

When the call was over, Jillian turned to her stepmother. "In all the craziness, we've forgotten Dad's birthday."

"I didn't," said Irene. "I bought him the most beautiful cashmere sweater weeks ago at Canali. It'll bring out the blue in his eyes."

"Good," said Jillian. "And you know what? I'm going to ask Piper if she can make a little birthday cake."

Irene looked skeptical. "I don't think he's going to feel much like observing his birthday."

"Maybe not," said Jillian as she stood up. "But it's more important than ever that he feels loved."

CHAPTER

98

THERE WERE THREE MESSAGES FROM her father. All of them announced that Vin and Terri wanted Piper to come home immediately. She didn't want to return the calls, but she knew that her parents would be beside themselves with worry.

When she reached her father, Piper led with the good news.

"I'm perfectly fine, Dad," she said. "And guess what? I got a commercial! It's shooting on Friday."

"Well, then, check out of Elysium and stay someplace else," Vin insisted.

"Look, Dad, I couldn't be safer. This place is swarming with police now."

It was also crossing Piper's mind that she didn't want to

spend her limited money on a second-rate hotel when she could stay free at luxurious Elysium. She assured her father she would check in frequently.

"Well, you know how I feel now, Piper. But you're a grown woman, and you're going to do what you want." Vin sighed. "Will you at least leave your phone on, lovey? It drives me crazy when I get that damned message."

As Piper promised, she heard a beep signaling another call. This time it was Jillian, asking if Piper could make a birthday cake.

"Something small," said Jillian. "It will only be my father, Irene, Ben, and me."

"Sure," said Piper. "Do you have a preference for cake, icing, colors, theme?"

"Oh, I don't know," said Jillian. "Surprise us. I'm sure whatever you come up with will be fine."

CHAPTER

99

BOOKING ON SUCH SHORT NOTICE, Jack had paid a fortune for the plane ticket. He was stuck in a middle seat, between a woman with a baby and a guy who smelled like he hadn't showered since Christmas. He hoped Piper would appreciate the heroics it had taken him to get to her side.

Jack was grateful his new boss was such a mensch. On extremely short notice, he'd agreed to letting Jack take today as a sick day and the following few days as annual leave. That was going to give Piper and him four whole days together. Jack hoped that when they came back east, they would have worked things out between them.

He'd debated letting Piper know he was coming but decided against it. Surprising her would be much more romantic—and he didn't want to give her a chance to tell him not to come.

Even if the romance didn't work out, this trip was not a waste. Jack wanted Piper to be safe. He didn't like her being in the middle of the mess at Elysium. The situation there had danger written all over it.

CHAPTER

100

W HY HAD HE EVEN COME to work today? He should have skipped out when he found the camera in Lillie Ulster's bag. How stupid he was. He'd walked right into this.

Kyle watched while the police searched the treatment room. As each drawer and cabinet was opened, he held his breath, praying that they didn't find his own secret camera. Folded towels and sheets were shaken open and thrown onto the floor. Bottles, jars, and tubes were tossed aside. Canisters of cotton pads, balls, and swabs were emptied.

"What have we here?" asked a cop, holding up a syringe and a bottle.

"Bag it," replied the detective.

As the search continued, Kyle began feeling hopeful that maybe they wouldn't find the camera after all. But when the detective's phone rang, Kyle sensed that the news wasn't going to be good. He wanted to smack the smug, self-satisfied expression off the dick's face as he listened to the caller.

"Oh, Kyle, Kyle, Kyle. What have you been doing, you naughty boy?" asked the detective when the phone call ended. "I hear you like going to the movies, don't you? My buddies just found a very interesting little video library at your apartment, you freakin' pervert."

CHAPTER

101

GRABBING THE PARCEL CONTAINING HER baking and decorating supplies, Piper exited her suite and took the elevator down. As she walked through the lobby on her way to the kitchen, she saw a crowd gathered outside in the courtyard. She went closer to the windows to get a better look at what was happening, but the people blocked her view. She went out the door, maneuvered through the onlookers, and managed to find a spot to stand.

Five police cars were parked, with lights flashing. A dozen officers stood waiting near the cars. Their eyes were fixed in the direction of the path that led to the skin-care center. Piper followed their gaze. Kyle Quigley, flanked by two more police officers, was walking toward the courtyard. His hands were behind his back, and his head was down.

The door of the first police car was opened. Before he got into the rear seat, Kyle looked up and scanned the crowd. Piper felt a chill as his eyes rested on her.

SHE KNEW HER MOTHER'S CHOCOLATE cake recipe by heart. Piper made a list of the ingredients and showed it to the chef.

"*Oui*," he said. "We have everything you need right here."

Within a few minutes, she stood in front of a worktable covered with all the cake makings. In a large bowl, she sifted together flour, sugar, cocoa powder, salt, and baking soda. Then, with an electric mixer, she blended in eggs, milk, canola oil, vanilla extract, and sour cream. After dividing the batter into cake pans, she slid them into the oven.

While she waited, Piper thought about how she would decorate the cake. Her mother used vanilla buttercream icing when she made the cake for The Icing on the Cupcake patrons. It was always a big seller. Might as well go for the surefire hit.

Her phone rang. It was Anastasia. Piper was apprehensive as she answered.

"The police just called. They want to come over and talk to me about Kyle Quigley. Anything you want to tell me, Piper?"

Piper swallowed and then spoke quickly. "I told them about Kyle and what you suspect, Anastasia. Lillie is dead, and somebody is trying to kill Jillian. The police should know everything so they can figure things out."

She held her breath as no sound came from Anastasia.

"I'm sorry, Anastasia, if I ruined your exclusive. I know how much energy you were putting in on it, but I couldn't just say nothing."

There was a pause. Finally Anastasia spoke. "Ah, don't worry about it, Piper. It would have been great to get the goods on Kyle Quigley myself, but I've already achieved what I wanted. My editor is so jazzed by the stuff I got on the fire and the murders that he's taking me off the Style beat. From now on, Anastasia Fernands is going to be covering hard news!"

CHAPTER

102

SISTER MARY NOELLE WELCOMED HER only sibling with a long, firm hug. "Thank the dear Lord that you are all right," she whispered.

"Oh, Nina, why is all this happening?" asked Jillian.

"I don't know. I don't know. We have to trust that God has his reasons."

"I wish I could be like you, Nina. I wish I could have such utter faith."

The two women walked to the garden and sat on a concrete bench.

"How do you think Daddy's handling everything?" asked Sister Mary Noelle.

"You know Daddy. He keeps it together on the outside, but all this has got to be killing him," said Jillian. "I'm glad that you reminded me about his birthday, though. I called Piper, and she's going to make a cake for him. Poor thing, I just threw the request at her, but I couldn't give her any suggestions on how to decorate it. Do you have any ideas?"

"Let's face it, Jillian, the thing that has always made Daddy happiest is you and me—at least until I entered the convent."

"And Mom," added Jillian. "I wish she were still here."

"Me, too," said Sister Mary Noelle. "But there's a perfect example. If our mother hadn't died, I wouldn't have been drawn to this life—away from everything that's needless and superficial. God had a plan."

Jillian was quiet as she thought about her sister's words.

"I have an idea," she said, suddenly brightening. "I know something that would be great on the top of Daddy's birthday cake."

She pulled out her cell phone.

CHAPTER

103

THE TOOTHPICK INSERTED INTO THE centers of the cakes came out clean. Piper took the pans from the oven and placed them on wire racks. While the layers were cooling, she mixed the buttercream icing. She wiped her hands on a towel as her phone rang again.

"Have you decorated the cake already?" asked Jillian.

"Not yet," said Piper.

"Well, I have an idea," said Jillian. "There's a picture of my father with my sister and me when we were little. It shows him sitting in a big wing chair with me in his lap and Nina perched on the arm of the chair. We're both watching as he reads us a book. Would there be any way you could re-create that picture on top of the cake?"

"If we had more time, we could have had the picture reproduced in edible ink," said Piper. "But I think I might be able to do it the old-fashioned way, by hand. I can use tracing paper to copy the picture and then go over the design to make an imprint on the cake."

"Great!" said Jillian, mustering up the first enthusiasm she'd felt in a long time. "The picture is in an album in my hope chest, which is in the garage at my father's house. I'll call Irene and let her know you're coming."

AFTER THE CAKE COOLED AND Piper frosted it, she asked for a tray to carry it over to the Abernathys' house. She packed her decorating paraphernalia and headed out of the kitchen. As she walked into the hallway, she almost collided with a thin, middle-aged man hurrying toward the lobby.

"Excuse me," said Piper, struggling to keep control of the tray. She looked at the man's pale face and remembered him. "Oh. Hi, Mr. Sherwood. How are you?"

"I'm going out to face the media hordes," said Hudson, shaking his head and frowning. "Vernon doesn't want to do it himself. He says I can handle it better than he can."

Though Piper detected some resentment in Hudson's tone, she also got the impression that he liked the idea of being the spokesperson for Elysium just fine.

"Wow, this is nuts," she said. "You just come back to

work and then get slammed with all this? When I met you last night at Jillian's, who could have guessed what was going to happen after you left?"

"Terrible, wasn't it? But now I can go out there and tell those media wolves that it's all over. Kyle Quigley is in police custody." Hudson looked down at his wrist. "Sorry. Got to fly," he said. "They're waiting for me."

Piper watched him hurry away. *That guy is actually loving all this.*

PIPER BALANCED THE CAKE TRAY while pushing the doorbell. The housekeeper answered. She was wearing rubber gloves and holding a sponge.

"Hi," said Piper. "Is Mrs. Abernathy here?"

"No," said the woman. "She was already gone when Miss Jillian called to say you would be here. Please, come in." She opened the door wider. "Can I help you with that?"

"No, no, I've got it. Thanks." Piper entered and followed the housekeeper to the kitchen, where she set the tray down on the counter.

"That's the door to the garage," said the housekeeper, pointing with her sponge. "The hope chest is against the far wall, covered with a blanket."

"Great," said Piper.

"Do you need anything else?" asked the housekeeper. "As soon as I finish cleaning the bathroom, I'm going to the market. So now's the time to ask."

"A couple of small bowls to mix colors into the icing," said Piper. "Other than that, I can't think of a thing."

PIPER SPREAD HER PIPING TIPS and disposable decorating bags on the counter. She split the icing she made in the Elysium kitchen into several bowls the housekeeper had brought her. Then she dropped yellow piping gel into the first bowl and folded it into the white frosting. No doubt she could use this color to simulate Jillian's hair—and maybe for her sister's, too. But before she could decide how to tint the rest of the icing, she had to see the picture.

As she walked to the garage door, the housekeeper appeared in the kitchen again. She had changed and was holding a set of car keys. "I'm leaving now," she said. "I'll go out with you."

As they entered the garage, the housekeeper gestured toward the far wall. "It's over there."

"Thanks," said Piper. She waited while the housekeeper got into one of the cars, backed out, and clicked the garage door closed.

CHAPTER

104

I N A SMALL ROOM WITH no windows, Kyle sat at a metal table while the detective interrogated him.

"That's some kinky stuff you got going there, Kyle. You've been up to no good, haven't you?"

Kyle didn't answer.

"You've got a regular library of your sick stunts. You should be congratulated for keeping it so organized and well labeled. We'll know exactly who to contact as prosecution witnesses."

The door to the interrogation room opened and a policewoman entered. She passed a folder to her colleague.

"Well, well, what do we have here?" asked the detective as he skimmed the folder's contents. "You've been busy at your computer, haven't you? We've got a list of all the porn sites you've visited."

Tapping his fingers on the table, Kyle didn't look at the detective.

"Okay, Kyle. We've got you nailed for sexual molestation. That could run you ten to fifteen years—for each case. But arson and murder—that clinches it." He pounded the table. "Put all that together and you'll be cooling your ass in Lancaster for the rest of your life."

"Wait a minute! Arson and murder?" Kyle exclaimed. His face was pale, and beads of perspiration had gathered on his forehead. "I didn't kill anybody! I swear!"

The detective ignored the denial. "Lancaster sure does attract a nice clientele," he continued. "Big Lurch spent some time there. Helluva guy. He tore open a woman's chest, took out her lung, and ate it. How'd you like a buddy like that as a roommate?"

"I want a lawyer," said Kyle as all remaining color drained from his face.

CHAPTER

105

GEORGE HAD HUMILIATED HIMSELF THE night before at Jillian's cottage, and he knew it. He had lain in bed all morning, nursing a hangover and feeling mortified. Finally he turned on the TV.

He felt some twisted satisfaction as he viewed the images of the charred remains of Jillian Abernathy's cottage, the glamorous head shot of Lillie Ulster, and clips from some of the roles she'd played. George had enjoyed the actress over the years in the movies and on television. It really was too bad that she'd been killed. But part of him was glad about the tragedies that were befalling Elysium.

Then his pulse began to race. He'd been at the cottage last night. He could be a suspect.

My God. Will they think that I did it?

The reporter stood in front of the Elysium gates as he wrapped up the story.

"Just a little while ago, police arrested thirty-six-year-old Kyle Quigley, a medical aesthetician here. Sources tell us that Quigley is suspected of having played a role in Lillic Ulster's death as well as in the attempted murder of Jillian Abernathy, the director of Elysium, this sprawling spa and cosmetic-surgery compound in the Hollywood Hills. Arraignment is expected to take place tomorrow. At that time we'll find out exactly what the charges against Quigley will be."

Breathing somewhat easier, George got out of bed. What was the matter with him? How had he become the sort of person who reveled in the downfall of others or could become a suspect in a murder investigation? How had be gotten to this place?

And what kind of example was he setting for Wendy? How were his reactions affecting his daughter? Though he tried not to show his anger and depression when he was with her, Wendy was very perceptive and sensitive. She had to sense his negative emotions, and that couldn't be helping her. The kid had a big fight on her hands. She needed support, not someone dragging her down.

Most of all she had to learn that when you experienced a tragedy, it was okay to lick your wounds for a while, but ultimately you had to keep going and do whatever it took to make the best of life.

As he got ready to take a shower, George came up with a plan. He was going to take Wendy to New York, or wherever the best plastic surgeons could be found. There had to be someone somewhere who could do the facial reconstruction she needed.

He didn't care how much it cost. His lawyer would make sure that Vernon Abernathy and his malpractice insurance paid. Elysium's owner would see that agreeing to a settlement was better than going to court and facing an even bigger judgment—not to mention all the negative publicity for the spa and his reputation.

George looked at the bloodshot eyes staring back at him in the bathroom mirror.

Sometimes, he thought, *you have to hit rock bottom to see your way up.*

CHAPTER

106

PULLING OFF THE BLANKET, PIPER looked at the large chest. The moth-repellent cedar sides were covered with painted angels, wedding bells, and stars. The chest was long and rectangular, reminding her of a casket. She sure wouldn't want something like this sitting in *her* marital bedroom.

Piper bent down to open the chest, fully expecting to be hit with the smell of cedar. Instead, as she raised the top, she inhaled the pungent aroma of turpentine.

CHAPTER

107

I HAVE SOMETHING I WANT TO show you, Jillian." Sister Mary Noelle reached into the pocket of her habit and pulled out an envelope. "I've been holding on to this since Mom died."

Jillian took the envelope from her sister, opened it, and began to read.

> *Dear Nina,*
>
> *Tomorrow morning I go in to have my face lift. As I write this, I think about my life and what has brought me to this point. Your father and I have had a very happy marriage, a fulfilling and loving life together. Our greatest joys have been you and Jillian. I couldn't have asked for more.*
>
> *I write this to you, Nina, because you've pleaded*

with me not to have this surgery. Jillian seems to understand, but you don't see why I am determined to take the risk. Shouldn't I be satisfied with the good fortune I've already enjoyed? Why does my physical appearance have to be so important? Why can't I come to terms with the aging process and accept it with grace?

I've tried, Nina, I truly have. In my heart I know you're right, but in my mind I know I will feel better if I look fresher and prettier. Sometimes I think when you've been physically blessed, it's harder to watch as your face deteriorates. It stings to hear people say, "She was so beautiful."

Jillian's eyes filled with tears. "This is breaking my heart," she whispered.

Sister Mary Noelle reached over and wrapped her arm around her sister's shoulder. Jillian sniffled and wiped at the corners of her eyes before she continued reading.

I know your father loves me, I do. But I want him to look at me the way he used to. I want him to be proud of his wife. I don't want to feel threatened by younger women.

If anything happens to me, I know your father will remarry. He should. He is an attractive, successful man. There is no shortage of women who would love it if I just disappeared.

Jillian paused. "Mom sure got *that* right," she said. "Irene wasn't the only Elysium employee who had her sights on Dad."

There was just one more paragraph left.

> *Please, Nina, if the day comes when your father needs to find another mate, be supportive. Having your approval will mean so much to him. Welcome her into the family, knowing that I've always wanted your father to be happy.*
>
> > *Love,*
> > *Mom*

Jillian put the letter down and looked at Sister Mary Noelle. "Why didn't you ever show me this?" she asked.

"Because it was painful for me. I wanted peace. Now I only feel guilty."

"About what?"

"That I could never find it in my heart to do as Mom asked. Even at the funeral, Irene was all over Daddy. God forgive me, I've never liked or trusted her."

"And why are you showing it to me now?" asked Jillian.

"Because I've prayed and prayed about this," answered Sister Mary Noelle. "I've prayed, ever since Mom died, that my negative feelings about Irene would prove to be unfounded. But with everything that's been happening at Elysium, I thought it was time."

CHAPTER

108

A PARTIALLY OPEN PLASTIC COOLER WAS in the hope chest. It was lying on top of a pile of fluffy white taffeta. Piper reached into the mound of material. She gasped as a pin pricked her finger.

A drop of blood appeared as she struggled to get her mind around what she was seeing. Was this Jillian's wedding dress? Why was it lying unaltered in the hope chest when, up until a couple of hours ago, the wedding was only a few days away?

CHAPTER

109

To avoid the media gathered at the front gate, Irene drove through the rear entrance. It was a crazy time for Elysium, but it would pass. Soon things would get back to normal and she would be the mistress of paradise again. She and Vernon would go on with their lives, and everything would be perfect.

The situation with Kyle Quigley had played right into her hands. The police assumed *he* had set the fire and murdered the actress. Tonight, when it was dark, she could take the flashlight from the hope chest and plant it someplace where it would incriminate Kyle. With the murder weapon, the police would have a virtually airtight case.

When enough time went by, she could take another stab at eliminating Jillian, just as she'd gotten rid of Jillian's mother. There was always that same method: pumping air into a vein and causing a fatal heart attack. A heart attack with no discernible cause.

As Irene pulled into the driveway and took from the car the additional birthday gift she'd bought for her husband, she still believed that ultimately *she* would be number one in Vernon's life.

CHAPTER

110

SOMETHING GLISTENED FROM INSIDE THE cooler. Piper pulled the handle open, peered in, and saw a heavy industrial flashlight. It was spattered with dark red spots. As she looked closer, Piper saw strands of long blond hair sticking to it. Her heart pounded as she realized that she was looking at the weapon used to beat in Lillie Ulster's head.

The pieces came rushing together in Piper's mind. Irene hadn't taken the dress to the bridal shop to be tailored because she didn't think there was *going* to be a wedding. Irene could have set the fire to make sure that Jillian would never be a bride.

But what about Lillie? Why would she be murdered? Had she witnessed Irene setting the fire? Did she have to be killed so she wouldn't be able to identify Irene as the arsonist?

CHAPTER

111

IRENE ENTERED THROUGH THE FRONT door. She set the brightly wrapped package on the coffee table in the living room and kicked off her shoes. Then she went to the kitchen.

Immediately she saw the cake and decorating supplies arrayed on the kitchen counter. Next her eyes turned to the door to the garage. It was slightly ajar.

She quietly slid open the kitchen drawer and selected the biggest knife there was before tiptoeing to the door and peeking. Her eyes swept over Vernon's Mercedes and came to rest on someone hunched over the hope chest.

"WHAT DO YOU THINK YOU'RE doing?"

Piper froze as she heard the voice.

"Get away from there!" Irene commanded. "Get away from there right now!"

Piper turned to face Irene as she tried to think what to do. Her means of escape were limited. The garage door was shut, and the button to open it was at the kitchen door. The only way out was past the woman standing in the doorway with a carving knife in her hand.

Irene stepped closer.

Then Piper had an idea. She inched toward the Mercedes that stood between her and Irene. In an instant she had opened the door, hopped inside, and quickly hit the button to lock the car.

She watched in terror as Irene ran toward the car and started pulling on the door handle. Her red face was twisted with rage. "Get out of that car!" Irene commanded. "Get out now." She was tugging at the door with such strength that the antitheft alarm was triggered.

The earsplitting sound of its angry blaring reverberated throughout the closed garage.

THE ALARM SYSTEM SENSED THAT the car was being tampered with and automatically sent a signal to the Mercedes-Benz response center. An automatically generated text message was immediately sent to Vernon Abernathy's cell phone, notifying him that his car was threatened.

IRENE'S EYES WIDENED AT THE sound of the insistent, blasting alarm. Why hadn't she demanded to have her own set of keys to Vernon's car? Then she'd simply be able to unlock the door and get to Piper.

She cast about wildly, looking around the garage for something—anything—that she could use to get inside the car.

There it was! Leaning against the wall.

She ran over to Vernon's golf bag and pulled out a driver.

VERNON READ THE TEXT MESSAGE. He wasn't really worried about theft. He knew that his car was safe. It was at home in the garage.

Maybe he should call home anyway, though, just to be sure everything was all right. He picked up the phone and punched in the numbers. As he listened to the continuing rings, he felt increasing frustration.

Why wasn't anyone picking up? He didn't need this at all. Didn't they know he already had enough to worry about?

THWACK!

Irene used all her strength, smashing the head of the golf club against the driver's-side window.

Terrified, Piper held her hands and forearms in front of her face and eyes, crouching low on the seat to shield herself from the glass she was sure was going to fly down on her. She listened to the pounding again as Irene slammed the metal driver against the glass. Eventually she heard a cracking sound.

God, help me!

Piper ventured a look. The glass had fractured, but the golf club hadn't broken through. That couldn't last much longer.

VERNON PULLED HIS HOUSE KEYS from his pocket and handed them to the security guard.

"The alarm in my car has activated. Can you please go over to the house and turn it off?"

As Piper looked up, she saw that the garage door's remote control was clipped to the visor over the steering wheel.

Thwack!

She then noticed a bulbous black key head protruding from the visor's edge. She reached out to pull down the visor, and the car key fell to the floor.

Jack claimed his bag at the carousel. The mild California air welcomed him as he walked outside the terminal to hail a cab. He was tempted to call Piper and tell her that he was there, but he decided he wanted to see her face when he surprised her.

"The Elysium Spa, please," he instructed the driver as he got into the taxi.

He had waited this long to see Piper. He could wait a little longer.

Piper pushed the remote button, and the garage door began to open. But what good was it unless she had the wherewithal to turn the car on and back out?

The key had fallen to the floor, but Piper couldn't see it from the crouched position she was in. She reached down and groped blindly, trying to find it. Finally the tips of her fingers touched it.

Focus. Focus. Don't look out at Irene. Focus.

She wrapped her fingers around the key, but as she lifted it, it hit the steering wheel and slipped out of her grasp.

Thwack! Thwack!

Piper was frantic. *Where is it? Where is it?*

She desperately felt along the car floor until she found the key again. The golf club came down hard against the glass as she started the ignition, shifted the car into reverse, and slammed her foot on the gas, tearing out of the garage.

EPILOGUE

PIPER HELD THE CELL PHONE to her ear with one hand while she threw clothes into her duffel bag with the other. She could hear Emmett barking in the background as she talked to her father.

"The director was a little psycho, but the shoot went really well today, Dad," said Piper. "The commercial will start airing in the spring and let's hope it gets lots of prime-time play so I make some money. And who knows? Some-body could see me in it and think of me for something else."

She looked over at Jack. He was lounging on the bed, watching her. She winked at him as she continued her phone conversation.

"Yes, I'm totally fine, Dad. I'm about to check out. Jack and I are going to take a ride up the coast to San Luis Obispo for the weekend. We have reservations to take the red-eye back home on Sunday night."

Though Piper was a bit apprehensive, she was excited about the trip. Being away from Jack and not talking to him had made her realize how much she missed him, how much he meant to her. When he showed up at Elysium, within an hour of her confrontation in the garage with Irene, Piper threw herself into his arms. He held her as she cried and comforted her while she poured out her story. Jack had guided and accompanied her through all the police questioning. Piper didn't know what she would have done without him.

"Please, Dad. You and Mom need to stop worrying," she said as she zipped the top of her bag. "It's all good. But I gotta go, Dad. I have one more thing to do for Jillian Abernathy."

SISTER MARY NOELLE SET OUT dozens of extra candles around the chapel. As she held a flame to each wick, she offered another prayer. She prayed for the souls of Esperanza Flores and Lillie Ulster, and she prayed for the living victims of Kyle Quigley.

Then Sister Mary Noelle said prayers of thanks. Jillian was safe and unharmed. So was their father. Irene was in police custody and would not be able to hurt anyone else. In addition to the incriminating evidence in the hope chest, the skin embedded beneath Esperanza's fingernails was being tested to see if it belonged to Irene.

The police had also taken Irene's computer and had discovered the Web sites she'd visited three years earlier with all the articles she'd accessed describing air embolisms as a cause of death and how to administer them without being detected. Sister Mary Noelle hoped that finally her father would stop blaming himself. He had nothing to do with her mother's death.

Irene would face legal justice. More important, God would judge her and hold her accountable for her sins.

The nun smiled as she walked to the back of the chapel to get an overview of how the place would look to Jillian when she walked down the candlelit aisle. On very short notice, the chancery office had granted permission for the wedding to take place here at the monastery. In front of God, family, and just a few close friends, Jillian and Ben were going to be married in this consecrated chapel by a priest, rather than in a gazebo with a justice of the peace.

God had answered Sister Mary Noelle's prayer.

THE TWO ROUND PUMPKIN LAYERS were baked, cooled, and waiting for Piper when she arrived at the Monastery of the Angels kitchen. She got to work immediately, spreading the cream-cheese icing before stacking them. When the entire cake was covered, white and smooth, Piper got out her piping tips and the containers of fondant and gum paste.

First she worked on making the wings, rolling out thin circles of gum paste, tracing her handmade pattern, and carefully cutting them out. Then she brushed the wings with silver luster dust and set them aside to dry.

The heads and bodies both were made with fondant. Piper rolled out small round balls and larger-size cones, fashioning the bottoms of the cones into the folds of flowing gowns. After making tiny indentations for eyes and mouths, she gently connected heads to bodies with toothpicks. She used edible glue to attach gum-paste arms to the sides of the angels' gowns, and then she attached the silvery wings to the angels' backs.

Taking an icing-filled decorating bag, she squeezed a zigzag edging around the base and another one on the top edge. Changing to tip #10, she placed hearts at precise intervals on the sides of the cake and the perimeter of the top layer, leaving a space in the middle. She gingerly set her angels in the center.

Standing back, Piper admired her work. She snapped a picture and posted it on Facebook along with her comment:

NOT TO PAT MYSELF ON THE BACK, BUT . . . LOOK AT THIS!

335

PIPER WALKED OUT OF THE convent and into the garden, where Jack was sitting on a concrete bench waiting for her.

"Okay, let's go," she said.

He nodded toward the chapel. "You're *sure* you don't want to go to the wedding?" he asked.

"No," Piper answered. "I'm ready to leave the City of Angels."

"You'll probably have to come back, you know," said Jack, "to testify in the trials."

She shrugged as she looked up at the Hollywood sign perched high up in the hills above the convent. "I hope I have lots of reasons to come back here," she said.

Hand in hand, they strolled to the parking lot.

Piper looked up into Jack's dark brown eyes. "Are you always going to play my knight in shining armor and come sweeping in to rescue me?" she asked.

"Only if you'll let me," he answered.

TERRI DONOVAN'S
ICING ON THE CUPCAKE
CREAM-CHEESE FROSTING

½ cup butter (1 stick), at room temperature
1½ cups cream cheese, also at room temperature
1 teaspoon vanilla
3 cups confectioners' sugar

Using an electric mixer at medium speed, beat the butter, cream cheese, and vanilla until smooth. Turn the mixer down to lowest speed and add the confectioners' sugar, a little at a time, until it's completely combined and smooth.

This recipe makes enough frosting for a triple-layer cake.

AUTHOR'S NOTE

THERE IS A REAL MONASTERY of the Angels. It is a cloistered convent that sits beneath the Hollywood sign in Los Angeles. To support themselves, the nuns do make the most delicious pumpkin bread, available to the public for purchase.

For more information, go to: www.themonasteryofthe angelslosangeles.com.

Sister Mary Noelle, Mother Mary Dominic, Sister Aloysius, and the things they say and do in this book are entirely the product of the author's imagination.

ACKNOWLEDGMENTS

ANGELS.

I'm a firm believer because I've experienced so many of them. Not the gauzy-gowned, golden-winged variety. I'm talking about the human ones that come, some utterly unexpected, and assist you through your life. Allow me to tell you about the angels that helped with *The Look of Love.*

A halo goes to Father Paul Holmes. Father Holmes has been on the job as I've written fourteen books now, supporting me and contributing his keen mind and rich imagination, along with a host of editorial skills. This is not the first time I've said it: Thank God for you, Paul.

Elizabeth Higgins Clark served as a fabulous guide in the City of Angels. Elizabeth, my actress daughter, is the inspiration for Piper Donovan. Elizabeth provides theatrical insights and makes sure Piper's voice is authentic.

Many thanks to Anastasia Fernands for supporting Cape Rep Theatre by purchasing a winning ticket and thus becoming a character in this book. My appreciation also goes to Michael Ghant for lending his name and, more important, for creating wonderful and inspirational programs for people with special needs. You are both angels.

Beth Tindall did a heavenly job as she redesigned www .maryjaneclark.com.

Two special angels continue to whisper in my ear. Jennifer Rudolph Walsh allows me to have my head in the clouds as she keeps her feet on the ground and expertly steers the business end of my writing career. Joni Evans, what can I say? Again and again, as busy as you are, you come through for me.

I'd like to take this opportunity to acknowledge the people at William Morrow/HarperCollins for their support and dedication. My insightful, creative editor Carrie Feron along with Lynn Grady, Jean Marie Kelly, Stephanie Kim, Michael Morrison, Shawn Nichols, Sharyn Rosenblum, Virginia Stanley, Liate Stehlick, and Tessa Woodward are a hardworking, professional team. Maureen Sugden is a dream of a copy editor. I realize there are so many others, unnamed here, who also contributed their publishing talents to bring this book to fruition.

Many, many thanks, my angels. This writer is blessed to have all of you.